THE HOBBIT
PART TWO

Robeltson
Aiden
P7

Aiden

By the same author:

The Lord of the Rings
The Silmarillion
Unfinished Tales
Farmer Giles of Ham
Roverandom
Letters from Father Christmas

THE HOBBIT
PART TWO

or

There and Back Again

J.R.R. TOLKIEN

with illustrations by
David Wyatt

HarperCollins *Children's Books*

First published in Great Britain by George Allen & Unwin 1937
This two-volume edition published in Great Britain by
HarperCollins *Children's Books* in 2012

HarperCollins *Children's Books* is a division of HarperCollins*Publishers* Ltd,
77-85 Fulham Palace Road, Hammersmith,
London, W6 8JB.

Visit our website at: www.harpercollins.co.uk

1

ISBN 978-0-00-792667-1

Printed and bound in England by Clays Ltd, St Ives plc

Contents

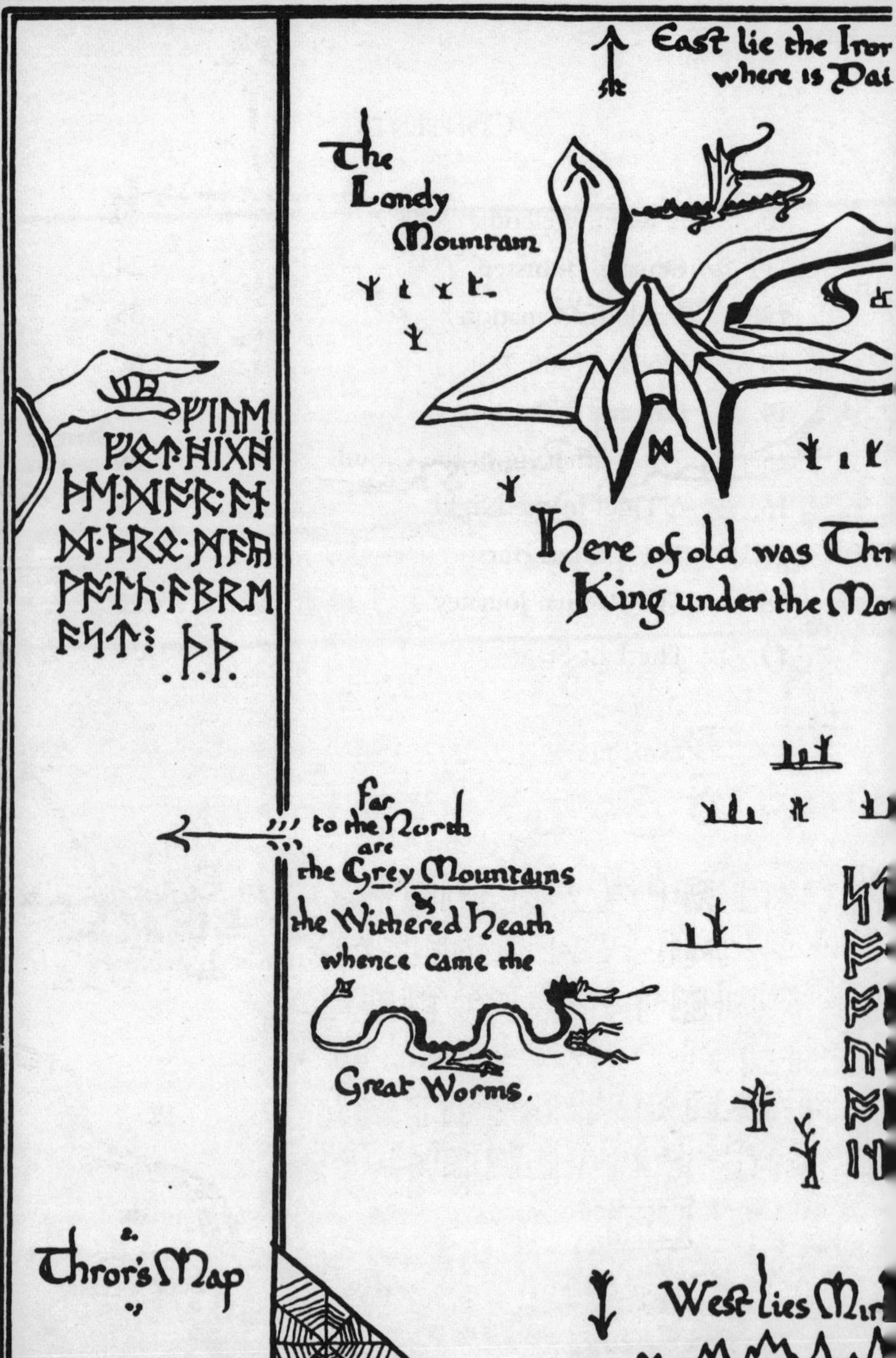
East lie the
where is
The Lonely Mountain
Here of old was
King under the
Far to the North are the Grey Mountains & the Withered Heath whence came the Great Worms.
Thror's Map
West lies

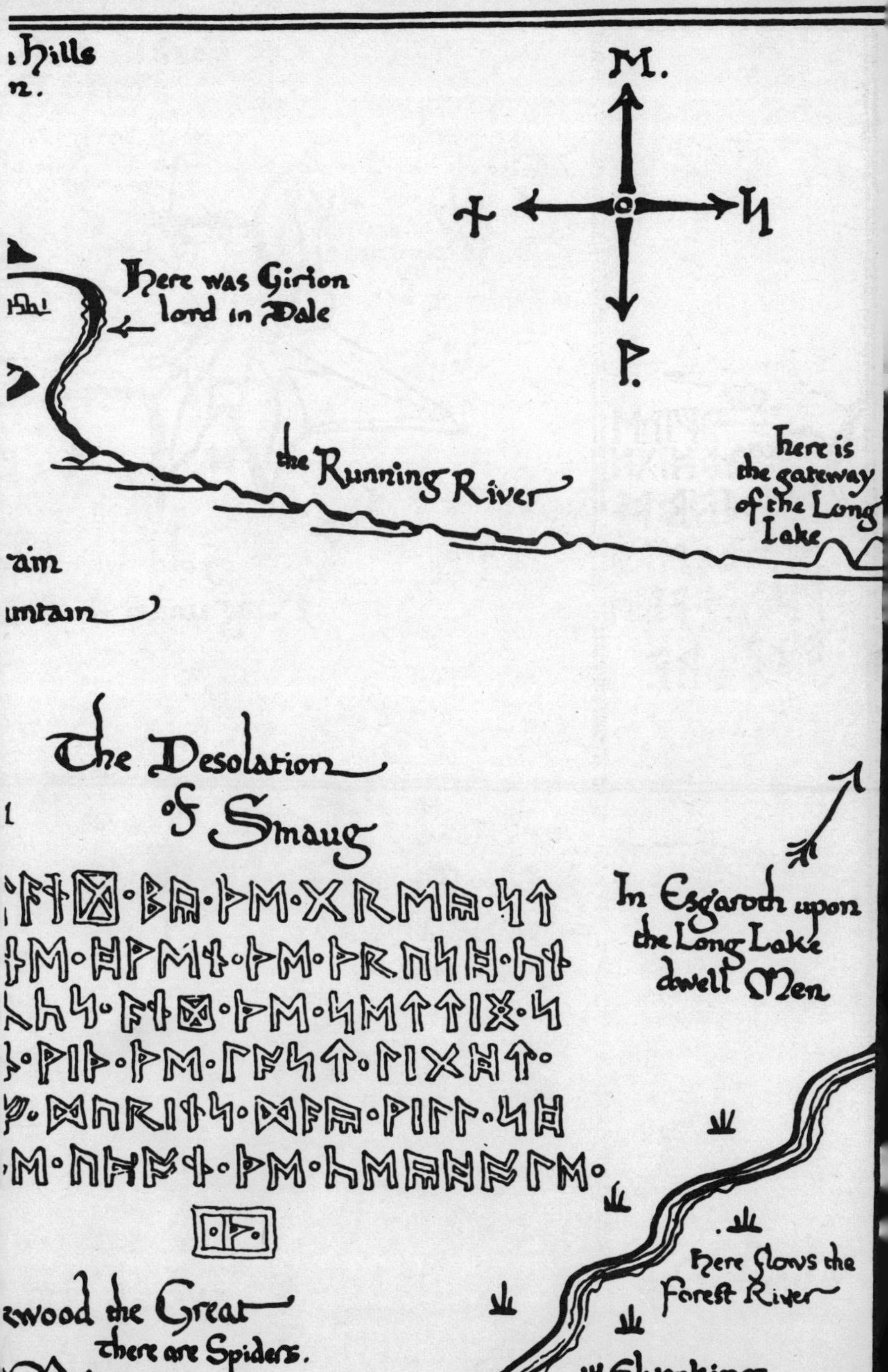

Hills
M.
P.
Here was Girion lord in Dale
the Running River
Here is the gateway of the Long Lake
The Desolation of Smaug
In Esgaroth upon the Long Lake dwell Men
Here flows the Forest River
wood the Great
there are Spiders.
Elvenking

Chapter 10

A Warm Welcome

THE DAY GREW lighter and warmer as they floated along. After a while the river rounded a steep shoulder of land that came down upon their left. Under its rocky feet like an inland cliff the deepest stream had flowed lapping and bubbling. Suddenly the cliff fell away. The shores sank. The trees ended. Then Bilbo saw a sight:

The lands opened wide about him, filled with the waters of the river which broke up and wandered in a hundred winding courses, or halted in marshes and pools dotted with isles on every side; but still a strong water flowed on steadily through the midst. And far away, its dark head in a torn cloud, there loomed the Mountain! Its nearest neighbours to the north-east and the tumbled land that joined it to them could not be seen. All alone it rose and looked across the marshes to the forest. The Lonely Mountain! Bilbo had come far and through many adventures to see it, and now he did not like the look of it in the least.

As he listened to the talk of the raft-men and pieced together the scraps of information they let fall, he soon realized that he was very fortunate ever to have seen it at all, even from this distance. Dreary as had been his imprisonment and unpleasant as was his position (to say nothing of the poor dwarves underneath him) still, he had been more lucky than he had guessed. The talk was all of the trade that came and went on the waterways and the growth of the traffic on the river, as the roads out of the East towards Mirkwood vanished or fell into disuse; and of the bickerings of the Lake-men and the Wood-elves about the upkeep of the Forest River and the care of the banks. Those lands had changed much since the days when dwarves dwelt in the Mountain, days which most people now remembered only as a very shadowy tradition. They had changed even in recent years, and since the last news that Gandalf had had of them. Great floods and rains had swollen the waters that flowed east; and there had been an earthquake or two (which some were inclined to attribute to the dragon – alluding to him chiefly with a curse and an ominous nod in the direction of the Mountain). The marshes and bogs had spread wider and wider on either side. Paths had vanished, and many a rider and wanderer too, if they had tried to find the lost ways across. The elf-road through the wood which the dwarves had followed on the advice of Beorn now came to a doubtful and little used end at the eastern edge of the forest; only the river offered any longer a safe way from the skirts of Mirkwood in the North to the mountain-shadowed plains beyond, and the river was guarded by the Wood-elves' king.

So you see Bilbo had come in the end by the only road that was any good. It might have been some comfort to Mr Baggins shivering on the barrels, if he had known that news of this had reached Gandalf far away and given him great anxiety, and that he was in fact finishing his other business (which does not come into this tale) and getting ready to come in search of Thorin's company. But Bilbo did not know it.

All he knew was that the river seemed to go on and on and on for ever, and he was hungry, and had a nasty cold in the nose, and did not like the way the Mountain seemed to frown at him and threaten him as it drew ever nearer. After a while, however, the river took a more southerly course and the Mountain receded again, and at last, late in the day the shores grew rocky, the river gathered all its wandering waters together into a deep and rapid flood, and they swept along at great speed.

The sun had set when turning with another sweep towards the east the Forest River rushed into the Long Lake. There it had a wide mouth with stony clifflike gates at either side whose feet were piled with shingles. The Long Lake! Bilbo had never imagined that any water that was not the sea could look so big. It was so wide that the opposite shores looked small and far, but it was so long that its northerly end, which pointed towards the Mountain, could not be seen at all. Only from the map did Bilbo know that away up there, where the stars of the Wain were already twinkling, the Running River came down into the lake from Dale and with the Forest River filled with deep waters what must once have been a great deep rocky valley. At the southern end the doubled waters poured out again over high waterfalls and ran away hurriedly to unknown lands. In the still evening air the noise of the falls could be heard like a distant roar.

Not far from the mouth of the Forest River was the strange town he heard the elves speak of in the king's cellars. It was not built on the shore, though there were a few huts and buildings there, but right out on the surface of the lake, protected from the swirl of the entering river by a promontory of rock which formed a calm bay. A great bridge made of wood ran out to where on huge piles made of forest trees was built a busy wooden town, not a town of elves but of Men, who still dared to dwell here under the shadow of the distant dragon-mountain. They still throve on the trade that came up the great river from the South and was carted past the falls to their town; but in the great days of old, when Dale in the North was rich and prosperous, they had been wealthy and powerful, and there had been fleets of boats on the waters, and some were filled with gold and some with warriors in armour, and there had been wars and deeds which were now only a legend. The rotting piles of a greater town could still be seen along the shores when the waters sank in a drought.

But men remembered little of all that, though some still

sang old songs of the dwarf-kings of the Mountain, Thror and Thrain of the race of Durin, and of the coming of the Dragon and the fall of the lords of Dale. Some sang too that Thror and Thrain would come back one day and gold would flow in rivers, through the mountain-gates, and all that land would be filled with new song and new laughter. But this pleasant legend did not much affect their daily business.

As soon as the raft of barrels came in sight boats rowed out from the piles of the town, and voices hailed the raft-steerers. Then ropes were cast and oars were pulled, and soon the raft was drawn out of the current of the Forest River and towed away round the high shoulder of rock into the little bay of Lake-town. There it was moored not far from the shoreward head of the great bridge. Soon men would come up from the South and take some of the casks away, and others they would fill with goods they had brought to be taken back up the stream to the Wood-elves' home. In the meantime the barrels were left afloat while the elves of the raft and the boatmen went to feast in Lake-town.

They would have been surprised, if they could have seen what happened down by the shore, after they had gone and the shades of night had fallen. First of all a barrel was cut loose by Bilbo and pushed to the shore and opened. Groans came from inside, and out crept a most unhappy dwarf. Wet straw was in his draggled beard; he was so sore and stiff, so bruised and buffeted he could hardly stand or stumble through the shallow water to lie groaning on the shore. He had a famished and a savage look like a dog that has been chained and forgotten in a kennel for a week. It was Thorin, but you could only have told it by his golden chain, and by the colour of his now dirty and tattered sky-blue hood with its tarnished silver tassel. It was some time before he would be even polite to the hobbit.

"Well, are you alive or are you dead?" asked Bilbo quite crossly. Perhaps he had forgotten that he had had at least one good meal more than the dwarves, and also the use of his arms and legs, not to speak of a greater allowance of air. "Are you still in prison, or are you free? If you want food, and if you want to go on with this silly adventure – it's yours after all and not mine – you had better slap your arms and rub your legs and try and help me get the others out while there is a chance!"

Thorin of course saw the sense of this, so after a few more groans he got up and helped the hobbit as well as he could. In the darkness floundering in the cold water they had a difficult and very nasty job finding which were the right barrels. Knocking outside and calling only discovered about six dwarves that could answer. These were unpacked and helped ashore where they sat or lay muttering and moaning; they were so soaked and bruised and scraped that they could hardly yet realise their release or be properly thankful for it.

Dwalin and Balin were two of the most unhappy, and it was no good asking them to help. Bifur and Bofur were less knocked about and drier, but they lay down and would do nothing. Fili and Kili, however, who were young (for dwarves) and had also been packed more neatly with plenty of straw into smaller casks, came out more or less smiling, with only a bruise or two and a stiffness that soon wore off.

"I hope I never smell the smell of apples again!" said Fili. "My tub was full of it. To smell apples everlastingly when you can scarcely move and are cold and sick with hunger is maddening. I could eat anything in the wide world now, for hours on end – but not an apple!"

With the willing help of Fili and Kili, Thorin and Bilbo at last discovered the remainder of the company and got them out. Poor fat Bombur was asleep or senseless; Dori, Nori, Ori, Oin and Gloin were waterlogged and seemed only half alive; they all had to be carried one by one and laid helpless on the shore.

"Well! Here we are!" said Thorin. "And I suppose we ought to thank our stars and Mr Baggins. I am sure he has a right to expect it, though I wish he could have arranged a more comfortable journey. Still – all very much at your service once more, Mr Baggins. No doubt we shall feel properly grateful, when we are fed and recovered. In the meanwhile, what next?"

"I suggest Lake-town," said Bilbo. "What else is there?"

Nothing else could, of course, be suggested; so leaving the others Thorin and Fili and Kili and the hobbit went along the shore to the great bridge. There were guards at the head of it, but they were not keeping very careful watch, for it was so long since there had been any real need. Except for occasional squabbles about river-tolls they were friends with the Wood-elves. Other folk were far away; and some of the younger people in the town openly doubted the existence of any dragon in the mountain, and laughed at the greybeards and gammers who said that they had seen him flying in the sky in their young days. That being so it is not surprising that the guards were drinking and laughing by a fire in their hut, and did not hear the noise of the unpacking of the dwarves or the footsteps of the four scouts. Their astonishment was enormous when Thorin Oakenshield stepped in through the door.

"Who are you and what do you want?" they shouted leaping to their feet and groping for weapons.

"Thorin son of Thrain son of Thror King under the Mountain!" said the dwarf in a loud voice, and he looked it, in spite of his torn clothes and draggled hood. The gold gleamed on his neck and waist; his eyes were dark and deep. "I have come back. I wish to see the Master of your town!"

Then there was tremendous excitement. Some of the more foolish ran out of the hut as if they expected the Mountain to go golden in the night and all the waters of the lake turn yellow right away. The captain of the guard came forward.

"And who are these?" he asked, pointing to Fili and Kili and Bilbo.

"The sons of my father's daughter," answered Thorin, "Fili and Kili of the race of Durin, and Mr Baggins who has travelled with us out of the West."

"If you come in peace lay down your arms!" said the captain.

"We have none," said Thorin, and it was true enough: their knives had been taken from them by the Wood-elves, and the great sword Orcrist too. Bilbo had his short sword, hidden as usual, but he said nothing about that. "We have no need of weapons, who return at last to our own as spoken of old. Nor could we fight against so many. Take us to your master!"

"He is at feast," said the captain.

"Then all the more reason for taking us to him," burst in Fili, who was getting impatient at these solemnities. "We are worn and famished after our long road and we have sick comrades. Now make haste and let us have no more words, or your master may have something to say to you."

"Follow me then," said the captain, and with six men about them he led them over the bridge through the gates and into the market-place of the town. This was a wide circle of quiet water surrounded by the tall piles on which were built the greater houses, and by long wooden quays with many steps and ladders going down to the surface of the lake. From one great hall shone many lights and there came the sound of many voices. They passed its doors and stood blinking in the light looking at long tables filled with folk.

"I am Thorin son of Thrain son of Thror King under the Mountain! I return!" cried Thorin in a loud voice from the door, before the captain could say anything.

All leapt to their feet. The Master of the town sprang from his great chair. But none rose in greater surprise than the raft-men of the elves who were sitting at the lower end of the hall. Pressing forward before the Master's table they cried:

"These are prisoners of our king that have escaped, wandering vagabond dwarves that could not give any good account of themselves, sneaking through the woods and molesting our people!"

"Is this true?" asked the Master. As a matter of fact he thought it far more likely than the return of the King under the Mountain, if any such person had ever existed.

"It is true that we were wrongfully waylaid by the Elvenking and imprisoned without cause as we journeyed back to our own land," answered Thorin. "But lock nor bar may hinder the homecoming spoken of old. Nor is this town in the Wood-elves' realm. I speak to the Master of the town of the Men of the lake, not to the raft-men of the king."

Then the Master hesitated and looked from one to the other. The Elvenking was very powerful in those parts and the Master wished for no enmity with him, nor did he think much of old songs, giving his mind to trade and tolls, to cargoes and gold, to which habit he owed his position. Others were of different mind, however, and quickly the matter was settled without him. The news had spread from the doors of the hall like fire through all the town. People were shouting inside the hall and outside it. The quays were thronged with hurrying feet. Some began to sing snatches of old songs concerning the return of the King under the Mountain; that it was Thror's grandson not Thror himself that had come back did not bother them at all. Others took up the song and it rolled loud and high over the lake.

The King beneath the mountains,
The King of carven stone,
The lord of silver fountains
Shall come into his own!

His crown shall be upholden,
His harp shall be restrung,
His halls shall echo golden
To songs of yore re-sung.

The woods shall wave on mountains
And grass beneath the sun;
His wealth shall flow in fountains
And the rivers golden run.

The streams shall run in gladness,
The lakes shall shine and burn,
All sorrow fail and sadness
At the Mountain-king's return!

So they sang, or very like that, only there was a great deal more of it, and there was much shouting as well as the music of harps and of fiddles mixed up with it. Indeed such excitement had not been known in the town in the memory of the oldest grandfather. The Wood-elves themselves began to wonder greatly and even to be afraid. They did not know of course how Thorin had escaped, and they began to think their king might have made a serious mistake. As for the

Master he saw there was nothing else for it but to obey the general clamour, for the moment at any rate, and to pretend to believe that Thorin was what he said. So he gave up to him his own great chair and set Fili and Kili beside him in places of honour. Even Bilbo was given a seat at the high table, and no explanation of where he came in – no songs had alluded to him even in the obscurest way – was asked for in the general bustle.

Soon afterwards the other dwarves were brought into the town amid scenes of astonishing enthusiasm. They were all doctored and fed and housed and pampered in the most delightful and satisfactory fashion. A large house was given up to Thorin and his company; boats and rowers were put at their service; and crowds sat outside and sang songs all day, or cheered if any dwarf showed so much as his nose.

Some of the songs were old ones; but some of them were quite new and spoke confidently of the sudden death of the dragon and of cargoes of rich presents coming down the river to Lake-town. These were inspired largely by the Master and they did not particularly please the dwarves, but in the meantime they were well contented and they quickly grew fat and strong again. Indeed within a week they were quite recovered, fitted out in fine cloth of their proper colours, with beards combed and trimmed, and proud steps. Thorin looked and walked as if his kingdom was already regained and Smaug chopped up into little pieces.

Then, as he had said, the dwarves' good feeling towards the little hobbit grew stronger every day. There were no more groans or grumbles. They drank his health, and they patted him on the back, and they made a great fuss of him; which was just as well, for he was not feeling particularly cheerful. He had not forgotten the look of the Mountain, nor the thought of the dragon, and he had beside a shocking cold. For three days he sneezed and coughed, and he could not go out, and even after that his speeches at banquets were limited to "Thag you very buch."

In the meanwhile the Wood-elves had gone back up the Forest River with their cargoes, and there was great excitement in the king's palace. I have never heard what happened to the chief of the guards and the butler. Nothing of course was ever said about keys or barrels while the dwarves stayed in Lake-town, and Bilbo was careful never to become invisible. Still, I daresay, more was guessed than was known, though doubtless Mr Baggins remained a bit of a mystery. In any case the king knew now the dwarves' errand, or thought he did, and he said to himself:

"Very well! We'll see! No treasure will come back through Mirkwood without my having something to say in the matter. But I expect they will all come to a bad end, and serve them right!" He at any rate did not believe in dwarves fighting and killing dragons like Smaug, and he strongly suspected attempted burglary or something like it – which shows he was a wise elf and wiser than the men of the town, though not quite right, as we shall see in the end. He sent out his spies about the shores of the lake and as far northward towards the Mountain as they would go, and waited.

At the end of a fortnight Thorin began to think of departure. While the enthusiasm still lasted in the town was the time to get help. It would not do to let everything cool down with delay. So he spoke to the Master and his councillors and said that soon he and his company must go on toward the Mountain.

Then for the first time the Master was surprised and a little frightened; and he wondered if Thorin was after all really a descendant of the old kings. He had never thought that the dwarves would actually dare to approach Smaug, but believed they were frauds who would sooner or later be discovered and be turned out. He was wrong. Thorin, of course, was really the grandson of the King under the Mountain, and there is no knowing what a dwarf will not dare and do for revenge or the recovery of his own.

But the Master was not sorry at all to let them go. They were expensive to keep, and their arrival had turned things into a long holiday in which business was at a standstill. "Let them go and bother Smaug, and see how he welcomes them!" he thought. "Certainly, O Thorin Thrain's son Thror's son!" was what he said. "You must claim your own. The hour is at hand, spoken of old. What help we can offer shall be yours, and we trust to your gratitude when your kingdom is regained."

So one day, although autumn was now getting far on, and winds were cold, and leaves were falling fast, three large boats left Lake-town, laden with rowers, dwarves, Mr Baggins, and many provisions. Horses and ponies had been sent round by circuitous paths to meet them at their appointed landing-place. The Master and his councillors bade them farewell from the great steps of the town-hall that went down to the lake. People sang on the quays and out of windows. The white oars dipped and splashed, off they went north up the lake on the last stage of their long journey. The only person thoroughly unhappy was Bilbo.

Chapter 11

ON THE DOORSTEP

IN TWO DAYS going they rowed right up the Long Lake and passed out into the River Running, and now they could all see the Lonely Mountain towering grim and tall before them. The stream was strong and their going was slow. At the end of the third day, some miles up the river, they drew in to the left or western bank and disembarked. Here they were joined by the horses with other provisions and necessaries and the ponies for their own use that had been sent to meet them. They packed what they could on the ponies and the rest was made into a store under a tent, but none of the men of the town would stay with them even for the night so near the shadow of the Mountain.

"Not at any rate until the songs have come true!" said they. It was easier to believe in the dragon and less easy to believe in Thorin in these wild parts. Indeed their stores had no need of any guard, for all the land was desolate and empty. So their escort left them, making off swiftly down the river and the shoreward paths, although the night was already drawing on.

They spent a cold and lonely night and their spirits fell. The next day they set off again. Balin and Bilbo rode behind, each leading another pony heavily laden beside him; the others were some way ahead picking out a low road, for there were no paths. They made north-west, slanting away from the River Running, and drawing ever nearer and nearer to a great spur of the Mountain that was flung out southwards towards them.

It was a weary journey, and a quiet and stealthy one. There was no laughter or song or sound of harps, and the pride and hopes which had stirred in their hearts at the singing of old songs by the lake died away to a plodding gloom. They knew that they were drawing near to the end of their journey, and that it might be a very horrible end. The land about them grew bleak and barren, though once, as Thorin told them, it had been green and fair. There was little grass, and before long there was neither bush nor tree, and only broken and blackened stumps to speak of ones long vanished. They were come to the Desolation of the Dragon, and they were come at the waning of the year.

They reached the skirts of the Mountain all the same without meeting any danger or any sign of the dragon other than the wilderness he had made about his lair. The Mountain lay dark and silent before them and ever higher above them. They made their first camp on the western side of the great southern spur, which ended in a height called Ravenhill. On this there had been an old watch-post; but they dared not climb it yet, it was too exposed.

Before setting out to search the western spurs of the Mountain for the hidden door, on which all their hopes rested, Thorin sent out a scouting expedition to spy out the land to the south where the Front Gate stood. For this purpose he chose Balin and Fili and Kili, and with them went Bilbo. They marched under the grey and silent cliffs to the feet of Ravenhill. There the river, after winding a wide loop over the valley of Dale, turned from the Mountain on its road to the Lake, flowing swift and noisily. Its bank was bare and rocky, tall and steep above the stream; and gazing out from it over the narrow water, foaming and splashing among many boulders, they could see in the wide valley shadowed by the Mountain's arms the grey ruins of ancient houses, towers, and walls.

"There lies all that is left of Dale," said Balin. "The mountain's sides were green with woods and all the sheltered valley rich and pleasant in the days when the bells rang in that town." He looked both sad and grim as he said this: he had been one of Thorin's companions on the day the dragon came.

They did not dare to follow the river much further towards the Gate; but they went on beyond the end of the southern spur, until lying hidden behind a rock they could look out and see the dark cavernous opening in a great cliff-wall between the arms of the Mountain. Out of it the waters of the Running River sprang; and out of it too there came a steam and a dark smoke. Nothing moved in the waste, save the vapour and the water, and every now and again a black and ominous crow. The only sound was the sound of the stony water, and every now and again the harsh croak of a bird. Balin shuddered.

"Let us return!" he said. "We can do no good here! And I don't like these dark birds, they look like spies of evil."

"The dragon is still alive and in the halls under the Mountain then – or I imagine so from the smoke," said the hobbit.

"That does not prove it," said Balin, "though I don't doubt you are right. But he might be gone away some time, or he might be lying out on the mountain-side keeping watch, and still I expect smokes and steams would come out of the gates: all the halls within must be filled with his foul reek."

With such gloomy thoughts, followed ever by croaking crows above them, they made their weary way back to the camp. Only in June they had been guests in the fair house of Elrond, and though autumn was now crawling towards winter that pleasant time now seemed years ago. They were alone in the perilous waste without hope of further help. They were at the end of their journey, but as far as ever, it seemed, from the end of their quest. None of them had much spirit left.

Now strange to say Mr Baggins had more than the others. He would often borrow Thorin's map and gaze at it, pondering over the runes and the message of the moon-letters Elrond had read. It was he that made the dwarves begin the dangerous search on the western slopes for the secret door. They moved their camp then to a long valley, narrower than the great dale in the south where the Gates of the river stood, and walled with lower spurs of the Mountain. Two of these here thrust forward west from the main mass in long steep-sided ridges that fell ever downwards towards the plain. On this western side there were fewer signs of the dragon's marauding feet, and there was some grass for their ponies. From this western camp, shadowed all day by cliff and wall until the sun began to sink towards the forest, day by day they toiled in parties searching for paths up the mountain-side. If the map was true, somewhere high above the cliff at the valley's head must stand the secret door. Day by day they came back to their camp without success.

But at last unexpectedly they found what they were seeking. Fili and Kili and the hobbit went back one day down the valley and scrambled among the tumbled rocks at its southern corner. About midday, creeping behind a great stone that stood alone like a pillar, Bilbo came on what looked like rough steps going upwards. Following these excitedly he and the dwarves found traces of a narrow track, often lost, often rediscovered, that wandered on to the top of the southern ridge and brought them at last to a still narrower ledge, which turned north across the face of the Mountain. Looking down they saw that they were at the top of the cliff at the valley's head, and were gazing down on to their own camp below. Silently, clinging to the rocky wall on their right, they went in single file along the ledge, till the wall opened and they turned into a little steep-walled bay, grassy-floored, still and quiet. Its entrance which they had found could not be seen from below because of the overhang of the cliff, nor from further off because it was so small that it looked like a dark crack and no more. It was not a cave and was open to the sky above; but at its inner end a flat wall rose up that in the lower part, close to the ground, was as smooth and upright as mason's work, but without a joint or crevice to be seen.

No sign was there of post or lintel or threshold, nor any sign of bar or bolt or keyhole; yet they did not doubt that they had found the door at last.

They beat on it, they thrust and pushed at it, they implored it to move, they spoke fragments of broken spells of opening, and nothing stirred. At last tired out they rested on the grass at its feet, and then at evening began their long climb down.

There was excitement in the camp that night. In the morning they prepared to move once more. Only Bofur and Bombur were left behind to guard the ponies and such stores as they had brought with them from the river. The others went down the valley and up the newly found path, and so to the narrow ledge. Along this they could carry no bundles or packs, so narrow and breathless was it, with a fall of a hundred and fifty feet beside them on to sharp rocks below; but each of them took a good coil of rope wound tight about his waist, and so at last without mishap they reached the little grassy bay.

There they made their third camp, hauling up what they needed from below with their ropes. Down the same way they were able occasionally to lower one of the more active dwarves, such as Kili, to exchange such news as there was, or to take a share in the guard below, while Bofur was hauled up to the higher camp. Bombur would not come up either the rope or the path.

"I am too fat for such fly-walks," he said. "I should turn dizzy and tread on my beard, and then you would be thirteen again. And the knotted ropes are too slender for my weight." Luckily for him that was not true, as you will see.

In the meanwhile some of them explored the ledge beyond the opening and found a path that led higher and higher on to the mountain; but they did not dare to venture very far that way, nor was there much use in it. Out up there a silence reigned, broken by no bird or sound except that of the wind in the crannies of stone. They spoke low and never called or sang, for danger brooded in every rock. The others who were busy with the secret of the door had no more success. They were too eager to trouble about the runes or the moon-letters, but tried without resting to discover where exactly in the smooth face of the rock the door was hidden. They had brought picks and tools of many sorts from Lake-town, and at first they tried to use these. But when they struck the stone the handles splintered and jarred their arms cruelly, and the steel heads broke or bent like lead. Mining work, they saw clearly, was no good against the magic that had shut this door; and they grew terrified, too, of the echoing noise.

Bilbo found sitting on the doorstep lonesome and wearisome – there was not a doorstep, of course, really, but they used to call the little grassy space between the wall and the opening the "doorstep" in fun, remembering Bilbo's words long ago at the unexpected party in his hobbit-hole, when he said they could sit on the doorstep till they thought of something. And sit and think they did, or wandered aimlessly about, and glummer and glummer they became.

Their spirits had risen a little at the discovery of the path, but now they sank into their boots; and yet they would not give it up and go away. The hobbit was no longer much brighter than the dwarves. He would do nothing but sit with his back to the rockface and stare away west through the opening, over the cliff, over the wide lands to the black wall of Mirkwood, and the distance beyond, in which he sometimes thought he could catch glimpses of the Misty Mountains small and far. If the dwarves asked him what he was doing he answered:

"You said sitting on the doorstep and thinking would be my job, not to mention getting inside, so I am sitting and thinking." But I am afraid he was not thinking much of the job, but of what lay beyond the blue distance, the quiet Western Land and the Hill and his hobbit-hole under it.

A large grey stone lay in the centre of the grass and he

stared moodily at it or watched the great snails. They seemed to love the little shut-in bay with its walls of cool rock, and there were many of them of huge size crawling slowly and stickily along its sides.

"Tomorrow begins the last week of autumn," said Thorin one day.

"And winter comes after autumn," said Bifur.

"And next year after that," said Dwalin, "and our beards will grow till they hang down the cliff to the valley before anything happens here. What is our burglar doing for us? Since he has got an invisible ring, and ought to be a specially excellent performer now, I am beginning to think he might go through the Front Gate and spy things out a bit!"

Bilbo heard this – the dwarves were on the rocks just above the enclosure where he was sitting – and "Good Gracious!" he thought, "so that is what they are beginning to think, is it? It is always poor me that has to get them out of their difficulties, at least since the wizard left. Whatever am I going to do? I might have known that something dreadful would happen to me in the end. I don't think I could bear to see the unhappy valley of Dale again, and as for that steaming gate!!!"

That night he was very miserable and hardly slept. Next day the dwarves all went wandering off in various directions; some were exercising the ponies down below, some were roving about the mountain-side. All day Bilbo sat gloomily in the grassy bay gazing at the stone, or out west through the narrow opening. He had a queer feeling that he was waiting for something. "Perhaps the wizard will suddenly come back today," he thought.

If he lifted his head he could see a glimpse of the distant forest. As the sun turned west there was a gleam of yellow upon its far roof, as if the light caught the last pale leaves. Soon he saw the orange ball of the sun sinking towards the level of his eyes. He went to the opening and there pale and faint was a thin new moon above the rim of the Earth.

At that very moment he heard a sharp crack behind him. There on the grey stone in the grass was an enormous thrush, nearly coal black, its pale yellow breast freckled with dark spots. Crack! It had caught a snail and was knocking it on the stone. Crack! Crack!

Suddenly Bilbo understood. Forgetting all danger he stood on the ledge and hailed the dwarves, shouting and waving. Those that were nearest came tumbling over the rocks and as fast as they could along the ledge to him, wondering what on earth was the matter; the others shouted to be hauled up the ropes (except Bombur, of course: he was asleep).

Quickly Bilbo explained. They all fell silent: the hobbit standing by the grey stone, and the dwarves with wagging beards watching impatiently. The sun sank lower and lower, and their hopes fell. It sank into a belt of reddened cloud and disappeared. The dwarves groaned, but still Bilbo stood almost without moving. The little moon was dipping to the horizon. Evening was coming on. Then suddenly when their hope was lowest a red ray of the sun escaped like a finger through a rent in the cloud. A gleam of light came straight through the opening into the bay and fell on the smooth rock-face. The old thrush, who had been watching from a high perch with beady eyes and head cocked on one side, gave a sudden trill. There was a loud crack. A flake of rock split from the wall and fell. A hole appeared suddenly about three feet from the ground.

Quickly, trembling lest the chance should fade, the dwarves rushed to the rock and pushed – in vain.

"The key! the key!" cried Bilbo. "Where is Thorin?"

Thorin hurried up.

"The key!" shouted Bilbo. "The key that went with the map! Try it now while there is still time!"

Then Thorin stepped up and drew the key on its chain from round his neck. He put it to the hole. It fitted and it turned! Snap! The gleam went out, the sun sank, the moon was gone, and evening sprang into the sky.

Now they all pushed together, and slowly a part of the rock-wall gave way. Long straight cracks appeared and widened. A door five feet high and three broad was outlined, and slowly without a sound swung inwards. It seemed as if darkness flowed out like a vapour from the hole in the mountain-side, and deep darkness in which nothing could be seen lay before their eyes, a yawning mouth leading in and down.

Chapter 12

INSIDE INFORMATION

FOR A LONG time the dwarves stood in the dark before the door and debated, until at last Thorin spoke:

"Now is the time for our esteemed Mr Baggins, who has proved himself a good companion on our long road, and a hobbit full of courage and resource far exceeding his size, and if I may say so possessed of good luck far exceeding the usual allowance – now is the time for him to perform the service for which he was included in our Company; now is the time for him to earn his Reward."

You are familiar with Thorin's style on important occasions, so I will not give you any more of it, though he went on a good deal longer than this. It certainly was an important occasion, but Bilbo felt impatient. By now he was quite familiar with Thorin too, and he knew what he was driving at.

"If you mean you think it is my job to go into the secret passage first, O Thorin Thrain's son Oakenshield, may your beard grow ever longer," he said crossly, "say so at once and have done! I might refuse. I have got you out of two messes already, which were hardly in the original bargain, so that I am, I think, already owed some reward. But 'third time pays for all' as my father used to say, and somehow I don't think I shall refuse. Perhaps I have begun to trust my luck more than I used to in the old days" – he meant last spring before he left his own house, but it seemed centuries ago – "but anyway I think I will go and have a peep at once and get it over. Now who is coming with me?"

He did not expect a chorus of volunteers, so he was not disappointed. Fili and Kili looked uncomfortable and stood on one leg, but the others made no pretence of offering – except old Balin, the look-out man, who was rather fond of the hobbit. He said he would come inside at least and perhaps a bit of the way too, ready to call for help if necessary.

The most that can be said for the dwarves is this: they intended to pay Bilbo really handsomely for his services; they had brought him to do a nasty job for them, and they did not mind the poor little fellow doing it if he would; but they would all have done their best to get him out of trouble, if he got into it, as they did in the case of the trolls at the beginning of their adventures before they had any particular reasons for being grateful to him. There it is: dwarves are not heroes, but calculating folk with a great idea of the value of money; some are tricky and treacherous and pretty bad lots; some are not, but are decent people like Thorin and Company, if you don't expect too much.

The stars were coming out behind him in a pale sky barred with black when the hobbit crept through the enchanted door and stole into the Mountain. It was far easier going than he expected. This was no goblin entrance, or rough wood-elves' cave. It was a passage made by dwarves, at the height of their wealth and skill: straight as a ruler, smooth-floored and smooth-sided, going with a gentle never-varying slope direct – to some distant end in the blackness below.

After a while Balin bade Bilbo "Good luck!" and stopped where he could still see the faint outline of the door, and by a trick of the echoes of the tunnel hear the rustle of the whispering voices of the others just outside. Then the hobbit slipped on his ring, and warned by the echoes to take more than hobbit's care to make no sound, he crept noiselessly down, down, down into the dark. He was trembling with fear, but his little face was set and grim. Already he was a very different hobbit from the one that had run out without a pocket-handkerchief from Bag-End long ago. He had not had a pocket-handkerchief for ages. He loosened his dagger in its sheath, tightened his belt, and went on.

"Now you are in for it at last, Bilbo Baggins," he said to himself. "You went and put your foot right in it that night of the party, and now you have got to pull it out and pay for it Dear me, what a fool I was and am!" said the least Tookish part of him. "I have absolutely no use for dragon-guarded treasures, and the whole lot could stay here for ever, if only I could wake up and find this beastly tunnel was my own front-hall at home!"

He did not wake up of course, but went still on and on, till all sign of the door behind had faded away. He was altogether alone. Soon he thought it was beginning to feel warm. "Is that a kind of a glow I seem to see coming right ahead down there?" he thought.

It was. As he went forward it grew and grew, till there was no doubt about it. It was a red light steadily getting redder and redder. Also it was now undoubtedly hot in the tunnel. Wisps of vapour floated up and past him and he began to sweat. A sound, too, began to throb in his ears, a sort of bubbling like the noise of a large pot galloping on the fire, mixed with a rumble as of a gigantic tom-cat purring. This grew to the unmistakable gurgling noise of some vast animal snoring in its sleep down there in the red glow in front of him.

It was at this point that Bilbo stopped. Going on from there was the bravest thing he ever did. The tremendous things that happened afterwards were as nothing compared to it. He fought the real battle in the tunnel alone, before he ever saw the vast danger that lay in wait. At any rate after a short halt go on he did; and you can picture him coming to the end of the tunnel, an opening of much the same size and shape as the door above. Through it peeps the hobbit's little head. Before him lies the great bottom-most cellar or dungeon-hall of the ancient dwarves right at the Mountain's root. It is almost dark so that its vastness can only be dimly guessed, but rising from the near side of the rocky floor there is a great glow. The glow of Smaug!

There he lay, a vast red-golden dragon, fast asleep; a thrumming came from his jaws and nostrils, and wisps of smoke, but his fires were low in slumber. Beneath him, under all his limbs and his huge coiled tail, and about him on all sides stretching away across the unseen floors, lay countless piles of precious things, gold wrought and unwrought, gems and jewels, and silver red-stained in the ruddy light.

Smaug lay, with wings folded like an immeasurable bat, turned partly on one side, so that the hobbit could see his underparts and his long pale belly crusted with gems and fragments of gold from his long lying on his costly bed. Behind him where the walls were nearest could dimly be seen coats of mail, helms and axes, swords and spears hanging; and there in rows stood great jars and vessels filled with a wealth that could not be guessed.

To say that Bilbo's breath was taken away is no description at all. There are no words left to express his staggerment, since Men changed the language that they learnt of elves in the days when all the world was wonderful. Bilbo had heard tell and sing of dragon-hoards before, but the splendour, the lust, the glory of such treasure had never yet come home to him. His heart was filled and pierced with enchantment and with the desire of dwarves; and he gazed motionless, almost forgetting the frightful guardian, at the gold beyond price and count.

* * *

He gazed for what seemed an age, before, drawn almost against his will, he stole from the shadow of the doorway, across the floor to the nearest edge of the mounds of treasure. Above him the sleeping dragon lay, a dire menace even in his sleep. He grasped a great two-handled cup, as heavy as he could carry, and cast one fearful eye upwards. Smaug stirred a wing, opened a claw, the rumble of his snoring changed its note.

Then Bilbo fled. But the dragon did not wake – not yet – but shifted into other dreams of greed and violence, lying there in his stolen hall while the little hobbit toiled back up the long tunnel. His heart was beating and a more fevered shaking was in his legs that when he was going down, but still he clutched the cup, and his chief thought was: "I've done it! This will show them. More like a grocer than a burglar, indeed! Well, we'll hear no more of that."

Nor did he. Balin was overjoyed to see the hobbit again, and as delighted as he was surprised. He picked Bilbo up and carried him out into the open air. It was midnight and clouds had covered the stars, but Bilbo lay with his eyes shut, gasping and taking pleasure in the feel of the fresh air again, and hardly noticing the excitement of the dwarves, or how they praised him and patted him on the back and put themselves and all their families for generations to come at his service.

The dwarves were still passing the cup from hand to hand and talking delightedly of the recovery of their treasure, when suddenly a vast rumbling woke in the mountain underneath as if it was an old volcano that had made up its mind to start eruptions once again. The door behind them was pulled nearly to, and blocked from closing with a stone, but up the long tunnel came the dreadful echoes, from far down in the depths, of a bellowing and a trampling that made the ground beneath them tremble.

Then the dwarves forgot their joy and their confident boasts of a moment before and cowered down in fright. Smaug was still to be reckoned with. It does not do to leave a live dragon out of your calculations, if you live near him. Dragons may not have much real use for all their wealth, but they know it to an ounce as a rule, especially after long possession; and Smaug was no exception. He had passed from an uneasy dream (in which a warrior, altogether insignificant in size but provided with a bitter sword and great courage, figured most unpleasantly) to a doze, and from a doze to wide waking. There was a breath of strange air in his cave. Could there be a draught from that little hole? He had never felt quite happy about it, though it was so small, and now he glared at it in suspicion and wondered why he had never blocked it up. Of late he had half fancied he had caught the dim echoes of a knocking sound from far above that came down through it to his lair. He stirred and stretched forth his neck to sniff. Then he missed the cup!

Thieves! Fire! Murder! Such a thing had not happened since first he came to the Mountain! His rage passes description – the sort of rage that is only seen when rich folk that have more than they can enjoy suddenly lose something that they have long had but have never before used or wanted. His fire belched forth, the hall smoked, he shook the mountain-roots. He thrust his head in vain at the little hole, and then coiling his length together, roaring like thunder underground, he sped from his deep lair through its great door, out into the huge passages of the mountain-palace and up towards the Front Gate.

To hunt the whole mountain till he had caught the thief and had torn and trampled him was his one thought. He issued from the Gate, the waters rose in fierce whistling steam, and up he soared blazing into the air and settled on the mountain-top in a spout of green and scarlet flame. The dwarves heard the awful rumour of his flight, and they crouched against the walls of the grassy terrace cringing under boulders, hoping somehow to escape the frightful eyes of the hunting dragon.

There they would have all been killed, if it had not been for Bilbo once again. "Quick! Quick!" he gasped. "The door! The tunnel! It's no good here."

Roused by these words they were just about to creep inside the tunnel when Bifur gave a cry: "My cousins! Bombur and Bofur – we have forgotten them, they are down in the valley!"

"They will be slain, and all our ponies too, and all our stores lost," moaned the others. "We can do nothing."

"Nonsense!" said Thorin, recovering his dignity. "We cannot leave them. Get inside Mr Baggins and Balin, and you two Fili and Kili – the dragon shan't have all of us. Now you others, where are the ropes? Be quick!"

Those were perhaps the worst moments they had been through yet. The horrible sounds of Smaug's anger were echoing in the stony hollows far above; at any moment he might come blazing down or fly whirling round and find them there, near the perilous cliff's edge hauling madly on the ropes. Up came Bofur, and still all was safe. Up came Bombur, puffing and blowing while the ropes creaked, and still all was safe. Up came some tools and bundles of stores, and then the danger was upon them.

A whirring noise was heard. A red light touched the points of standing rocks. The dragon came.

They had barely time to fly back to the tunnel, pulling and dragging in their bundles, when Smaug came hurtling from the North, licking the mountain-sides with flame, beating his great wings with a noise like a roaring wind. His hot breath shrivelled the grass before the door, and drove in through the crack they had left and scorched them as they lay hid. Flickering fires leapt up and black rock-shadows danced. Then darkness fell as he passed again. The ponies screamed with terror, burst their ropes and galloped wildly off. The dragon swooped and turned to pursue them, and was gone.

"That'll be the end of our poor beasts!" said Thorin. "Nothing can escape Smaug once he sees it. Here we are and here we shall have to stay, unless any one fancies tramping the long open miles back to the river with Smaug on the watch!"

It was not a pleasing thought! They crept further down the tunnel, and there they lay and shivered though it was warm and stuffy, until dawn came pale through the crack of the door. Every now and again through the night they could hear the roar of the flying dragon grow and then pass and fade, as he hunted round and round the mountain-sides.

He guessed from the ponies, and from the traces of the camps he had discovered, that men had come up from the river and the lake and had scaled the mountain-side from the valley where the ponies had been standing; but the door withstood his searching eye, and the little high-walled bay had kept out his fiercest flames. Long he had hunted in vain till the dawn chilled his wrath and he went back to his golden couch to sleep – and to gather new strength. He would not forget or forgive the theft, not if a thousand years turned him to smouldering stone, but he could afford to wait. Slow and silent he crept back to his lair and half closed his eyes.

When morning came the terror of the dwarves grew less. They realized that dangers of this kind were inevitable in dealing with such a guardian, and that it was no good giving up their quest yet. Nor could they get away just now, as Thorin had pointed out. Their ponies were lost or killed, and they would have to wait some time before Smaug relaxed his watch sufficiently for them to dare the long way on foot. Luckily they had saved enough of their stores to last them still for some time.

They debated long on what was to be done, but they could think of no way of getting rid of Smaug – which had always been a weak point in their plans, as Bilbo felt inclined to point out. Then as is the nature of folk that are thoroughly perplexed, they began to grumble at the hobbit, blaming him for what had at first so pleased them: for bringing away a cup and stirring up Smaug's wrath so soon.

"What else do you suppose a burglar is to do?" asked Bilbo angrily. "I was not engaged to kill dragons, that is warrior's work, but to steal treasure. I made the best beginning I could. Did you expect me to trot back with the whole hoard of Thror on my back? If there is any grumbling to be done, I think I might have a say. You ought to have brought five hundred burglars not one. I am sure it reflects great credit on your grandfather, but you cannot pretend that you ever made the vast extent of his wealth clear to me. I should want hundreds of years to bring it all up, if I was fifty times as big, and Smaug as tame as a rabbit."

After that of course the dwarves begged his pardon. "What then do you propose we should do, Mr Baggins?" asked Thorin politely.

"I have no idea at the moment – if you mean about removing the treasure. That obviously depends entirely on some new turn of luck and the getting rid of Smaug. Getting rid of dragons is not at all in my line, but I will do my best to think about it. Personally I have no hopes at all, and wish I was safe back at home."

"Never mind that for the moment! What are we to do now, today?"

"Well, if you really want my advice, I should say we can

do nothing but stay where we are. By day we can no doubt creep out safely enough to take the air. Perhaps before long one or two could be chosen to go back to the store by the river and replenish our supplies. But in the meanwhile everyone ought to be well inside the tunnel by night.

"Now I will make you an offer. I have got my ring and will creep down this very noon – then if ever Smaug ought to be napping – and see what he is up to. Perhaps something will turn up. 'Every worm has his weak spot,' as my father used to say, though I am sure it was not from personal experience."

Naturally the dwarves accepted the offer eagerly. Already they had come to respect little Bilbo. Now he had become the real leader in their adventure. He had begun to have ideas and plans of his own. When midday came he got ready for another journey down into the Mountain. He did not like it of course, but it was not so bad now he knew, more or less, what was in front of him. Had he known more about dragons and their wily ways, he might have been more frightened and less hopeful of catching this one napping.

The sun was shining when he started, but it was as dark as night in the tunnel. The light from the door, almost closed, soon faded as he went down. So silent was his going that smoke on a gentle wind could hardly have surpassed it, and he was inclined to feel a bit proud of himself as he drew near the lower door. There was only the very faintest glow to be seen.

"Old Smaug is weary and asleep," he thought. "He can't

see me and he won't hear me. Cheer up, Bilbo!" He had forgotten or had never heard about dragons' sense of smell. It is also an awkward fact that they can keep half an eye open watching while they sleep, if they are suspicious.

Smaug certainly looked fast asleep, almost dead and dark, with scarcely a snore more than a whiff of unseen steam, when Bilbo peeped once more from the entrance. He was just about to step out on to the floor when he caught a sudden thin and piercing ray of red from under the drooping lid of Smaug's left eye. He was only pretending to sleep! He was watching the tunnel entrance! Hurriedly Bilbo stepped back and blessed the luck of his ring. Then Smaug spoke.

"Well, thief! I smell you and I feel your air. I hear your breath. Come along! Help yourself again, there is plenty and to spare!"

But Bilbo was not quite so unlearnt in dragon-lore as all that, and if Smaug hoped to get him to come nearer so easily he was disappointed. "No thank you, O Smaug the Tremendous!" he replied. "I did not come for presents. I only wished to have a look at you and see if you were truly as great as tales say. I did not believe them."

"Do you now?" said the dragon, somewhat flattered, even though he did not believe a word of it.

"Truly songs and tales fall utterly short of the reality, O Smaug the chiefest and Greatest of Calamities," replied Bilbo.

"You have nice manners for a thief and a liar," said the dragon. "You seem familiar with my name, but I don't seem to remember smelling you before. Who are you and where do you come from, may I ask?"

"You may indeed! I come from under the hill, and under the hills and over the hills my paths led. And through the air. I am he that walks unseen."

"So I can well believe," said Smaug, "but that is hardly your usual name."

"I am the clue-finder, the web-cutter, the stinging fly. I was chosen for the lucky number."

"Lovely titles!" sneered the dragon. "But lucky numbers don't always come off."

"I am he that buries his friends alive and drowns them and draws them alive again from the water. I came from the end of a bag, but no bag went over me.

"These don't sound so creditable," scoffed Smaug.

"I am the friend of bears and the guest of eagles. I am Ring-winner and Luckwearer; and I am Barrel-rider," went on Bilbo beginning to be pleased with his riddling.

"That's better!" said Smaug. "But don't let your imagination run away with you!"

This of course is the way to talk to dragons, if you don't want to reveal your proper name (which is wise), and don't want to infuriate them by a flat refusal (which is also very wise). No dragon can resist the fascination of riddling talk and of wasting time trying to understand it. There was a lot here which Smaug did not understand at all (though I expect you do, since you know all about Bilbo's adventures to which he was referring), but he thought he understood enough, and he chuckled in his wicked inside.

"I thought so last night," he smiled to himself. "Lake-men, some nasty scheme of those miserable tub-trading Lake-men, or I'm a lizard. I haven't been down that way for an age and an age; but I will soon alter that!"

"Very well, O Barrel-rider!" he said aloud. "Maybe Barrel was your pony's name; and maybe not, though it was fat enough. You may walk unseen, but you did not walk all the way. Let me tell you I ate six ponies last night and I shall catch and eat all the others before long. In return for the excellent meal I will give you one piece of advice for your good; don't have more to do with dwarves than you can help!"

"Dwarves!" said Bilbo in pretended surprise.

"Don't talk to me!" said Smaug. "I know the smell (and taste) of dwarf – no one better. Don't tell me that I can eat a dwarf-ridden pony and not know it! You'll come to a bad end, if you go with such friend, Thief Barrel-rider. I don't mind if you go back and tell them so from me." But he did not tell Bilbo that there was one smell he could not make out at all, hobbit-smell; it was quite outside his experience and puzzled him mightily.

"I suppose you got a fair price for that cup last night?" he went on. "Come now, did you? Nothing at all! Well, that's just like them. And I suppose they are skulking outside, and your job is to do all the dangerous work and get what you can when I'm not looking – for them? And you will get a fair share? Don't you believe it! If you get off alive, you will be lucky."

★ ★ ★

Bilbo was now beginning to feel really uncomfortable. Whenever Smaug's roving eye, seeking for him in the shadows, flashed across him, he trembled, and an unaccountable desire seized hold of him to rush out and reveal himself and tell all the truth to Smaug. In fact he was in grievous danger of coming under the dragon-spell. But plucking up courage he spoke again.

"You don't know everything, O Smaug the Mighty," said he. "Not gold alone brought us hither."

"Ha! Ha! You admit the 'us'," laughed Smaug. "Why not say 'us fourteen' and be done with it, Mr Lucky Number? I am pleased to hear that you had other business in these parts besides my gold. In that case you may, perhaps, not altogether waste your time.

"I don't know if it has occurred to you that, even if you could steal the gold bit by bit – a matter of a hundred years or so – you could not get it very far? Not much use on the mountain-side? Not much use in the forest? Bless me! Had you never thought of the catch? A fourteenth share, I suppose, or something like it, those were the terms, eh? But what about delivery? What about cartage? What about armed guards and tolls?" And Smaug laughed aloud. He had a wicked and a wily heart, and he knew his guesses were not far out, though he suspected that the Lake-men were at the back of the plans, and that most of the plunder was meant to stop there in the town by the shore that in his young days had been called Esgaroth.

You will hardly believe it, but poor Bilbo was really very

taken aback. So far all his thoughts and energies had been concentrated on getting to the Mountain and finding the entrance. He had never bothered to wonder how the treasure was to be removed, certainly never how any part of it that might fall to his share was to be brought back all the way to Bag-End, Underhill.

Now a nasty suspicion began to grow in his mind – had the dwarves forgotten this important point too, or were they laughing in their sleeves at him all the time? That is the effect that dragon-talk has on the inexperienced. Bilbo of course ought to have been on his guard; but Smaug had rather an overwhelming personality.

"I tell you," he said, in an effort to remain loyal to his friends and to keep his end up, "that gold was only an afterthought with us. We came over hill and under hill, by wave and wind, for *Revenge*. Surely, O Smaug the unassessably wealthy, you must realize that your success has made you some bitter enemies?"

Then Smaug really did laugh – a devastating sound which shook Bilbo to the floor, while far up in the tunnel the dwarves huddled together and imagined that the hobbit had come to a sudden and a nasty end.

"Revenge!" he snorted, and the light of his eyes lit the hall from floor to ceiling like scarlet lightning. "Revenge! The King under the Mountain is dead and where are his kin that dare seek revenge? Girion Lord of Dale is dead, and I have eaten his people like a wolf among sheep, and where are his sons' sons that dare approach me? I kill where I wish and none dare resist. I laid low the warriors of old and their like is not in the world today. Then I was but young and tender. Now I am old and strong, strong, strong, Thief in the Shadows!" he gloated. "My armour is like tenfold shields, my teeth are swords, my claws spears, the shock of my tail a thunderbolt, my wings a hurricane, and my breath death!"

"I have always understood," said Bilbo in a frightened squeak, "that dragons were softer underneath, especially in the region of the – er – chest; but doubtless one so fortified has thought of that."

The dragon stopped short in his boasting. "Your information is antiquated," he snapped. "I am armoured above and below with iron scales and hard gems. No blade can pierce me."

"I might have guessed it," said Bilbo. "Truly there can nowhere be found the equal of Lord Smaug the Impenetrable. What magnificence to possess a waistcoat of fine diamonds!"

"Yes, it is rare and wonderful, indeed," said Smaug absurdly pleased. He did not know that the hobbit had already caught a glimpse of his peculiar under-covering on his previous visit, and was itching for a closer view for reasons of his own. The dragon rolled over. "Look!" he said. "What do you say to that?"

"Dazzlingly marvellous! Perfect! Flawless! Staggering!" exclaimed Bilbo aloud, but what he thought inside was: "Old fool! Why there is a large patch in the hollow of his left breast as bare as a snail out of its shell!"

After he had seen that Mr Baggins' one idea was to get

away. "Well, I really must not detain Your Magnificence any longer," he said, "or keep you from much needed rest. Ponies take some catching, I believe, after a long start. And so do burglars," he added as a parting shot, as he darted back and fled up the tunnel.

It was an unfortunate remark, for the dragon spouted terrific flames after him, and fast though he sped up the slope, he had not gone nearly far enough to be comfortable before the ghastly head of Smaug was thrust against the opening behind. Luckily the whole head and jaws could not squeeze in, but the nostrils sent forth fire and vapour to pursue him, and he was nearly overcome, and stumbled blindly on in great pain and fear. He had been feeling rather pleased with the cleverness of his conversation with Smaug, but his mistake at the end shook him into better sense.

"Never laugh at live dragons, Bilbo you fool!" he said to himself, and it became a favourite saying of his later, and passed into a proverb. "You aren't nearly through this adventure yet," he added, and that was pretty true as well.

The afternoon was turning into evening when he came out again and stumbled and fell in a faint on the "doorstep". The dwarves revived him, and doctored his scorches as well as they could; but it was a long time before the hair on the back of his head and his heels grew properly again: it had all been singed and frizzled right down to the skin. In the meanwhile his friends did their best to cheer him up; and they were eager for his story, especially wanting to know why the dragon had made such an awful noise, and how Bilbo had escaped.

But the hobbit was worried and uncomfortable, and they had difficulty in getting anything out of him. On thinking things over he was now regretting some of the things he had said to the dragon, and was not eager to repeat them. The old thrush was sitting on a rock near by with his head cocked on one side, listening to all that was said. It shows what an ill temper Bilbo was in: he picked up a stone and threw it at the thrush, which merely fluttered aside and came back.

"Drat the bird!" said Bilbo crossly. "I believe he is listening, and I don't like the look of him."

"Leave him alone!" said Thorin. "Thrushes are good and friendly – this is a very old bird indeed, and is maybe the last left of the ancient breed that used to live about here, tame to the hands of my father and grandfather. They were a long-lived and magical race, and this might even be one of those that were alive then, a couple of hundreds of years or more ago. The Men of Dale used to have the trick of understanding their language, and used them for messengers to fly to the Men of the Lake and elsewhere."

"Well, he'll have news to take to Lake-town all right, if that is what he is after," said Bilbo; "though I don't suppose there are any people left there that trouble with thrush-language."

"Why what has happened?" cried the dwarves. "Do get on with your tale!"

So Bilbo told them all he could remember, and he confessed that he had a nasty feeling that the dragon guessed too much from his riddles added to the camps and the ponies.

"I am sure he knows we came from Lake-town and had help from there; and I have a horrible feeling that his next move may be in that direction. I wish to goodness I had never said that about Barrel-rider; it would make even a blind rabbit in these parts think of the Lake-men."

"Well, well! It cannot be helped, and it is difficult not to slip in talking to a dragon, or so I have always heard," said Balin anxious to comfort him. "I think you did very well, if you ask me – you found out one very useful thing at any rate, and got home alive, and that is more than most can say who have had words with the likes of Smaug. It may be a mercy and a blessing yet to know of the bare patch in the old Worm's diamond waistcoat."

That turned the conversation, and they all began discussing dragon-slayings historical, dubious, and mythical, and the various sorts of stabs and jabs and undercuts, and the different arts, devices and stratagems by which they had been accomplished. The general opinion was that catching a dragon napping was not as easy as it sounded, and the attempt to stick one or prod one asleep was more likely to end in disaster than a bold frontal attack. All the while they talked the thrush listened, till at last when the stars began to peep forth, it silently spread its wings and flew away. And all the while they talked and the shadows lengthened Bilbo became more and more unhappy and his forebodings grew.

At last he interrupted them. "I am sure we are very unsafe here," he said, "and I don't see the point of sitting here. The dragon has withered all the pleasant green, and anyway the night has come and it is cold. But I feel it in my bones that this place will be attacked again. Smaug knows now how I came down to his hall, and you can trust him to guess where the other end of the tunnel is. He will break all this side of the Mountain to bits, if necessary, to stop up our entrance, and if we are smashed with it the better he will like it."

"You are very gloomy, Mr Baggins!" said Thorin. "Why has not Smaug blocked the lower end, then, if he is so eager to keep us out? He has not, or we should have heard him."

"I don't know, I don't know – because at first he wanted to try and lure me in again, I suppose, and now perhaps because he is waiting till after tonight's hunt, or because he does not want to damage his bedroom if he can help it – but I wish you would not argue. Smaug will be coming out at any minute now, and our only hope is to get well in the tunnel and shut the door."

He seemed so much in earnest that the dwarves at last did as he said, though they delayed shutting the door – it seemed a desperate plan, for no one knew whether or how they could get it open again from the inside, and the thought of being shut in a place from which the only way out led through the dragon's lair was not one they liked. Also everything seemed quite quiet, both outside and down the tunnel. So for a longish while they sat inside not far down from the half-open door and went on talking.

The talk turned to the dragon's wicked words about the dwarves. Bilbo wished he had never heard them, or at least that he could feel quite certain that the dwarves now were absolutely honest when they declared that they had never thought at all about what would happen after the treasure had been won. "We knew it would be a desperate venture," said Thorin, "and we know that still; and I still think that when we have won it will be time enough to think what to do about it. As for your share, Mr Baggins, I assure you we are more than grateful and you shall choose your own fourteenth, as soon as we have anything to divide. I am sorry if you are worried about transport, and I admit the difficulties are great – the lands have not become less wild with the passing of time, rather the reverse – but we will do whatever we can for you, and take our share of the cost when the time comes. Believe me or not as you like!"

From that the talk turned to the great hoard itself and to the things that Thorin and Balin remembered. They wondered if they were still lying there unharmed in the hall below: the spears that were made for the armies of the great King Bladorthin (long since dead) each had a thrice-forged head and their shafts were inlaid with cunning gold, but they were never delivered or paid for; shields made for warriors long dead; the great golden cup of Thror, two-handed, hammered and carven with birds and flowers whose eyes and petals were of jewels; coats of mail gilded and silvered and impenetrable; the necklace of Girion, Lord of Dale, made of five hundred emeralds green as grass, which he gave for the arming of his eldest son in a coat of dwarf-linked rings the like of which had never been made before, for it was wrought of pure silver to the power and strength of triple steel. But fairest of all was the great white gem, which the dwarves had found beneath the roots of the Mountain, the Heart of the Mountain, the Arkenstone of Thrain.

"The Arkenstone! The Arkenstone!" murmured Thorin in the dark, half dreaming with chin upon his knees.

"It was like a globe with a thousand faces; it shone like silver in the firelight, like water in the sun, like snow under the stars, like rain upon the Moon!"

But the enchanted desire of the hoard had fallen from Bilbo. All through their talk he was only half listening to them. He sat nearest to the door with one ear cocked for any beginnings of a sound without, his other was alert for echoes beyond the murmurs of the dwarves, for any whisper of a movement from far below.

Darkness grew deeper and he grew ever more uneasy. "Shut the door!" he begged them, "I fear that dragon in my marrow. I like this silence far less than the uproar of last night. Shut the door before it is too late!"

Something in his voice gave the dwarves an uncomfortable feeling. Slowly Thorin shook off his dreams and getting up he kicked away the stone that wedged the door. Then they thrust upon it, and it closed with a snap and a clang. No trace of a keyhole was there left on the inside. They were shut in the Mountain!

And not a moment too soon. They had hardly gone any distance down the tunnel when a blow smote the side of the Mountain like the crash of battering-rams made of forest oaks and swung by giants. The rock boomed, the walls cracked and stones fell from the roof on their heads. What would have happened if the door had still been open I don't like to think. They fled further down the tunnel glad to be still alive, while behind them outside they heard the roar and rumble of Smaug's fury. He was breaking rocks to pieces, smashing wall and cliff with the lashings of his huge tail, till their little lofty camping ground, the scorched grass, the thrush's stone, the snail-covered walls, the narrow ledge, and all disappeared in a jumble of smithereens, and an avalanche of splintered stones fell over the cliff into the valley below.

Smaug had left his lair in silent stealth, quietly soared into the air, and then floated heavy and slow in the dark like a monstrous crow, down the wind towards the west of the Mountain, in the hopes of catching unawares something or somebody there, and of spying the outlet to the passage which the thief had used. This was the outburst of his wrath when he could find nobody and see nothing, even where he guessed the outlet must actually be.

After he had let off his rage in this way he felt better and he thought in his heart that he would not be troubled again from that direction. In the meanwhile he had further vengeance to take. "Barrel-rider!" he snorted. "Your feet came from the waterside and up the water you came without a doubt. I don't know your smell, but if you are not one of those men of the Lake, you had their help. They shall see me and remember who is the real King under the Mountain!"

He rose in fire and went away south towards the Running River.

Chapter 13

Not at Home

In the meanwhile, the dwarves sat in darkness, and utter silence fell about them. Little they ate and little they spoke. They could not count the passing of time; and they scarcely dared to move, for the whisper of their voices echoed and rustled in the tunnel. If they dozed, they woke still to darkness and to silence going on unbroken. At last after days and days of waiting, as it seemed, when they were becoming choked and dazed for want of air, they could bear it no longer. They would almost have welcomed sounds from below of the dragon's return. In the silence they feared some cunning devilry of his, but they could not sit there for ever.

Thorin spoke: "Let us try the door!" he said. "I must feel the wind on my face soon or die. I think I would rather be smashed by Smaug in the open than suffocate in here!" So several of the dwarves got up and groped back to where the door had been.

But they found that the upper end of the tunnel had been shattered and blocked with broken rock. Neither key nor the magic it had once obeyed would ever open that door again.

"We are trapped!" they groaned. "This is the end. We shall die here."

But somehow, just when the dwarves were most despairing, Bilbo felt a strange lightening of the heart, as if a heavy weight had gone from under his waistcoat.

"Come, come!" he said. " 'While there's life there's hope!' as my father used to say, and 'Third time pays for all.' I am going *down* the tunnel once again. I have been that way twice, when I knew there was a dragon at the other end, so I will risk a third visit when I am no longer sure. Anyway the only way out is down. And I think this time you had better all come with me."

In desperation they agreed, and Thorin was the first to go forward by Bilbo's side.

"Now do be careful!" whispered the hobbit, "and as quiet as you can be! There may be no Smaug at the bottom, but then again there may be. Don't let us take any unnecessary risks!"

Down, down they went. The dwarves could not, of course, compare with the hobbit in real stealth, and they made a deal of puffing and shuffling which echoes magnified alarmingly, but though every now and again Bilbo in fear stopped and listened, not a sound stirred below. Near the bottom, as well as he could judge, Bilbo slipped on his ring and went ahead. But he did not need it: the darkness was complete, and they were all invisible, ring or no ring. In fact so black was it that the hobbit came to the opening unexpectedly, put his hand on air, stumbled forward, and rolled headlong into the hall!

There he lay face downwards on the floor and did not dare to get up, or hardly even to breathe. But nothing moved. There was not a gleam of light – unless, as it seemed to him, when at last he slowly raised his head, there was a pale white glint, above him and far off in the gloom. But certainly it was not a spark of dragon-fire, though the worm-stench was heavy in the place, and the taste of vapour was on his tongue.

At length Mr Baggins could bear it no longer, "Confound you, Smaug, you worm!" he squeaked aloud. "Stop playing hide-and-seek! Give me a light, and then eat me, if you can catch me!"

Faint echoes ran round the unseen hall, but there was no answer.

Bilbo got up, and found that he did not know in what direction to turn.

"Now I wonder what on earth Smaug is playing at," he said. "He is not at home today (or tonight, or whatever it is), I do believe. If Oin and Gloin have not lost their tinder-boxes, perhaps we can make a little light, and have a look round before the luck turns."

"Light!" he cried. "Can anybody make a light?"

The dwarves, of course, were very alarmed when Bilbo fell forward down the step with a bump into the hall, and they sat huddled just where he had left them at the end of the tunnel.

"Sh! sh!" they hissed, when they heard his voice; and though that helped the hobbit to find out where they were, it was some time before he could get anything else out of them. But in the end, when Bilbo actually began to stamp on the floor, and screamed out "light!" at the top of his shrill voice, Thorin gave way, and Oin and Gloin were sent back to their bundles at the top of the tunnel.

After a while a twinkling gleam showed them returning, Oin with a small pine-torch alight in his hand, and Gloin with a bundle of others under his arm. Quickly Bilbo trotted to the door and took the torch; but he could not persuade the dwarves to light the others or to come and join him yet. As Thorin carefully explained, Mr Baggins was still officially their expert burglar and investigator. If he liked to risk a light, that was his affair. They would wait in the tunnel for his report. So they sat near the door and watched.

They saw the little dark shape of the hobbit start across the floor holding his tiny light aloft. Every now and again, while he was still near enough, they caught a glint and a tinkle as he stumbled on some golden thing. The light grew smaller as he wandered away into the vast hall; then it began to rise dancing into the air. Bilbo was climbing the great mound of treasure. Soon he stood upon the top, and still went on. Then they saw him halt and stoop for a moment; but they did not know the reason.

It was the Arkenstone, the Heart of the Mountain. So Bilbo guessed from Thorin's description; but indeed there could not be two such gems, even in so marvellous a hoard, even in all the world. Ever as he climbed the same white gleam had shone before him and drawn his feet towards it.

Slowly it grew to a little globe of pallid light. Now as he came near, it was tinged with a flickering sparkle of many colours at the surface, reflected and splintered from the wavering light of his torch. At last he looked down upon it and he caught his breath. The great jewel shone before his feet of its own inner light, and yet, cut and fashioned by the dwarves, who had dug it from the heart of the mountain long ago, it took all light that fell upon it and changed it into ten thousand sparks of white radiance shot with glints of the rainbow.

Suddenly Bilbo's arm went towards it drawn by its enchantment. His small hand would not close about it, for it was a large and heavy gem; but he lifted it, shut his eyes, and put it in his deepest pocket.

"Now I am a burglar indeed!" thought he. "But I suppose I must tell the dwarves about it – some time. They did say I could pick and choose my own share; and I think I would choose this, if they took all the rest!" All the same he had an uncomfortable feeling that the picking and choosing had not really been meant to include this marvellous gem, and that trouble would yet come of it.

Now he went on again. Down the other side of the great mound he climbed, and the spark of his torch vanished from the sight of the watching dwarves. But soon they saw it far away in the distance again. Bilbo was crossing the floor of the hall.

He went on, until he came to the great doors at the further side, and there a draught of air refreshed him, but it almost puffed out his light. He peeped timidly through, and caught a glimpse of great passages and of the dim beginnings of wide stairs going up into the gloom. And still there was no sight nor sound of Smaug. He was just going to turn and go back, when a black shape swooped at him, and brushed his face. He squeaked and stared, stumbled backwards and fell. His torch dropped head downwards and went out!

"Only a bat, I suppose and hope!" he said miserably. "But now what am I do do? Which is East, South, North, or West?"

"Thorin! Balin! Oin! Gloin! Fili! Kili!" he cried as loud as he could – it seemed a thin little noise in the wide blackness. "The light's gone out! Someone come and find me and help me!" For the moment his courage had failed altogether.

Faintly the dwarves heard his small cries, though the only word they could catch was "help!"

"Now what on earth or under it has happened?" said Thorin. "Certainly not the dragon, or he would not go on squeaking."

They waited a moment or two, and still there were no dragon-noises, no sound at all in fact but Bilbo's distant voice. "Come, one of you, get another light or two!" Thorin ordered. "It seems we have got to go and help our burglar."

"It is about our turn to help," said Balin, "and I am quite willing to go. Anyway I expect it is safe for the moment."

Gloin lit several more torches, and then they all crept out, one by one, and went along the wall as hurriedly as they could. It was not long before they met Bilbo himself coming back towards them. His wits had quickly returned as soon as he saw the twinkle of their lights.

"Only a bat and a dropped torch, nothing worse!" he said in answer to their questions. Though they were much relieved, they were inclined to be grumpy at being frightened for nothing; but what they would have said, if he had told them at that moment about the Arkenstone, I don't know. The mere fleeting glimpses of treasure which they had caught as they went along and rekindled all the fire of their dwarvish hearts; and when the heart of a dwarf, even the most respectable, is wakened by gold and by jewels, he grows suddenly bold, and he may become fierce.

The dwarves indeed no longer needed any urging. All were now eager to explore the hall while they had the chance, and willing to believe that, for the present, Smaug was away from home. Each now gripped a lighted torch; and as they gazed, first on one side and then on another, they forgot fear and even caution. They spoke aloud, and cried out to one another, as they lifted old treasures from the mound or from the wall and held them in the light, caressing and fingering them.

Fili and Kili were almost in merry mood, and finding still hanging there many golden harps strung with silver they took them and struck them; and being magical (and also untouched by the dragon, who had small interest in music) they were still in tune. The dark hall was filled with melody that had long been silent. But most of the dwarves were more practical: they gathered gems and stuffed their pockets, and let what they could not carry fall back through their fingers with a sigh. Thorin was not least among these; but always he searched from side to side for something which he could not find. It was the Arkenstone; but he spoke of it yet to no one.

Now the dwarves took down mail and weapons from the walls, and armed themselves. Royal indeed did Thorin look, clad in a coat of gold-plated rings, with a silver-hafted axe in a belt crusted with scarlet stones.

"Mr Baggins!" he cried. "Here is the first payment of your reward! Cast off your old coat and put on this!"

With that he put on Bilbo a small coat of mail, wrought for some young elf-prince long ago. It was of silver-steel, which the elves call *mithril*, and with it went a belt of pearls and crystals. A light helm of figured leather strengthened beneath with hoops of steel, and studded about the brim with white gems, was set upon the hobbit's head.

"I feel magnificent," he thought; "but I expect I look rather absurd. How they would laugh on the Hill at home! Still I wish there was a looking-glass handy!"

All the same Mr Baggins kept his head more clear of the bewitchment of the hoard than the dwarves did. Long before the dwarves were tired of examining the treasures, he became weary of it and sat down on the floor; and he began to wonder nervously what the end of it all would be. "I would give a good many of these precious goblets," he thought, "for a drink of something cheering out of one of Beorn's wooden bowls!"

"Thorin!" he cried aloud. "What next? We are armed, but what good has any armour ever been before against Smaug the Dreadful? This treasure is not yet won back. We are not looking for gold yet, but for a way of escape; and we have tempted luck too long!"

"You speak the truth!" answered Thorin, recovering his wits. "Let us go! I will guide you. Not in a thousand years should I forget the ways of this palace." Then he hailed the others, and they gathered together, and holding their torches above their heads they passed through the gaping doors, not without many a backward glance of longing.

Their glittering mail they had covered again with their old cloaks and their bright helms with their tattered hoods, and one by one they walked behind Thorin, a line of little lights in the darkness that halted often, listening in fear once more for any rumour of the dragon's coming.

Though all the old adornments were long mouldered or destroyed, and though all was befouled and blasted with the comings and goings of the monster, Thorin knew every passage and every turn. They climbed long stairs, and turned and went down wide echoing ways, and turned again and climbed yet more stairs, and yet more stairs again. These were smooth, cut out of the living rock broad and fair; and up, up, the dwarves went, and they met no sign of any living thing, only furtive shadows that fled from the approach of their torches fluttering in the draughts.

The steps were not made, all the same, for hobbit-legs, and Bilbo just was feeling that he could go on no longer, when suddenly the roof sprang high and far beyond the reach of their torch-light. A white glimmer could be seen coming through some opening far above, and the air smelt sweeter. Before them light came dimly through great doors, that hung twisted on their hinges and half burnt.

"This is the great chamber of Thror," said Thorin; "the hall of feasting and of council. Not far off now is the Front Gate."

They passed through the ruined chamber. Tables were rotting there; chairs and benches were lying there overturned, charred and decaying. Skulls and bones were upon the floor among flagons and bowls and broken drinking-horns and dust. As they came through yet more doors at the further end, a sound of water fell upon their ears, and the grey light grew suddenly more full.

"There is the birth of the Running River," said Thorin. "From here it hastens to the Gate. Let us follow it!"

Out of a dark opening in a wall of rock there issued a boiling water, and it flowed swirling in a narrow channel, carved and made straight and deep by the cunning of ancient hands. Beside it ran a stone-paved road, wide enough for many men abreast. Swiftly along this they ran, and round a wide-sweeping turn – and behold! before them stood the broad light of day. In front there rose a tall arch, still showing the fragments of old carven work within, worn and splintered and blackened though it was. A misty sun sent its pale light between the arms of the Mountain, and beams of gold fell on the pavement at the threshold.

A whirl of bats frightened from slumber by their smoking torches flurried over them; as they sprang forward their feet slithered on stones rubbed smooth and slimed by the passing of the dragon. Now before them the water fell noisily outward and foamed down towards the valley. They flung their pale torches to the ground, and stood gazing out with dazzled eyes. They were come to the Front Gate, and were looking out upon Dale.

"Well!" said Bilbo, "I never expected to be looking *out* of this door. And I never expected to be so pleased to see the sun again, and to feel the wind on my face. But, ow! this wind is cold!"

It was. A bitter easterly breeze blew with a threat of oncoming winter. It swirled over and round the arms of the Mountain into the valley, and sighed among the rocks. After their long time in the stewing depths of the dragon-haunted caverns, they shivered in the sun.

Suddenly Bilbo realized that he was not only tired but also very hungry indeed. "It seems to be late morning," he said, "and so I suppose it is more or less breakfast-time – if there is any breakfast to have. But I don't feel that Smaug's front doorstep is the safest place for a meal. Do let's go somewhere where we can sit quiet for a bit!"

"Quite right!" said Balin. "And I think I know which way we should go: we ought to make for the old look-out post at the south-west corner of the Mountain."

"How far is that?" asked the hobbit.

"Five hours march, I should think. It will be rough going. The road from the Gate along the left edge of the stream seems all broken up. But look down there! The river loops suddenly east across Dale in front of the ruined town. At that point there was once a bridge, leading to steep stairs that climbed up the right bank, and so to a road running towards Ravenhill. There is (or was) a path that left the road and climbed up to the post. A hard climb, too, even if the old steps are still there."

"Dear me!" grumbled the hobbit. "More walking and more climbing without breakfast! I wonder how many breakfasts, and other meals, we have missed inside that nasty clockless, timeless hole?"

As a matter of fact two nights and the day between had gone by (and not altogether without food) since the dragon smashed the magic door, but Bilbo had quite lost count, and it might have been one night or a week of nights for all he could tell.

"Come, come!" said Thorin laughing – his spirits had begun to rise again, and he rattled the precious stones in his pockets. "Don't call my palace a nasty hole! You wait till it has been cleaned and redecorated!"

"That won't be till Smaug's dead," said Bilbo glumly. "In the meanwhile where is he? I would give a good breakfast to know. I hope he is not up on the Mountain looking down at us!"

That idea disturbed the dwarves mightily, and they quickly decided that Bilbo and Balin were right.

"We must move away from here," said Dori. "I feel as if his eyes were on the back of my head."

"It's a cold lonesome place," said Bombur. "There may be drink, but I see no sign of food. A dragon would always be hungry in such parts."

"Come on! Come on!" cried the others. "Let us follow Balin's path!"

Under the rocky wall to the right there was no path, so on they trudged among the stones on the left side of the river, and the emptiness and desolation soon sobered even Thorin again. The bridge that Balin had spoken of they found long fallen, and most of its stones were now only boulders in the shallow noisy stream; but they forded the water without much difficulty, and found the ancient steps, and climbed the high bank. After going a short way they struck the old road, and before long came to a deep dell sheltered among the rocks; there they rested for a while and had such a breakfast as they could, chiefly *cram* and water. (If you want to know what *cram* is, I can only say that I don't know the recipe; but it is biscuitish, keeps good indefinitely, is supposed to be sustaining, and is certainly not entertaining, being in fact very uninteresting except as a chewing exercise. It was made by the Lake-men for long journeys.)

After that they went on again; and now the road struck westwards and left the river, and the great shoulder of the south-pointing mountain-spur drew ever nearer. At length they reached the hill path. It scrambled steeply up, and they plodded slowly one behind the other, till at last in the late afternoon they came to the top of the ridge and saw the wintry sun going downwards to the West.

Here they found a flat place without a wall on three sides, but backed to the North by a rocky face in which there was an opening like a door. From that door there was a wide view East and South and West.

"Here," said Balin, "in the old days we used always to keep watchmen, and that door behind leads into a rock-hewn chamber that was made here as a guardroom. There were several places like it round the Mountain. But there seemed small need for watching in the days of our prosperity, and the guards were made over comfortable, perhaps – otherwise we might have had longer warning of the coming of the dragon, and things might have been different. Still, here we can now lie hid and sheltered for a while, and can see much without being seen."

"Not much use, if we have been seen coming here," said Dori, who was always looking up towards the Mountain's peak, as if he expected to see Smaug perched there like a bird on a steeple.

"We must take our chance of that," said Thorin. "We can go no further today."

"Hear, hear!" cried Bilbo, and flung himself on the ground.

In the rock-chamber there would have been room for a hundred, and there was a small chamber further in, more removed from the cold outside. It was quite deserted; not even wild animals seemed to have used it in all the days of Smaug's dominion. There they laid their burdens; and some threw themselves down at once and slept, but the others sat near the outer door and discussed their plans. In all their talk they came perpetually back to one thing: where was Smaug? They looked West and there was nothing, and East there was nothing, and in the South there was no sign of the dragon, but there was a gathering of very many birds. At that they gazed and wondered; but they were no nearer understanding it, when the first cold stars came out.

Chapter 14

FIRE AND WATER

NOW IF YOU wish, like the dwarves, to hear news of Smaug, you must go back again to the evening when he smashed the door and flew off in rage, two days before.

The men of the lake-town Esgaroth were mostly indoors, for the breeze was from the black East and chill, but a few were walking on the quays, and watching, as they were fond of doing, the stars shine out from the smooth patches of the lake as they opened in the sky. From their town the Lonely Mountain was mostly screened by the low hills at the far end of the lake, through a gap in which the Running River came down from the North. Only its high peak could they see in clear weather, and they looked seldom at it, for it was ominous and drear even in the light of morning. Now it was lost and gone, blotted in the dark.

Suddenly it flickered back to view; a brief glow touched

it and faded.

"Look!" said one. "The lights again! Last night the watchmen saw them start and fade from midnight until dawn. Something is happening up there."

"Perhaps the King under the Mountain is forging gold," said another. "It is long since he went north. It is time the songs began to prove themselves again."

"Which king?" said another with a grim voice. "As like as not it is the marauding fire of the dragon, the only king under the Mountain we have ever known."

"You are always foreboding gloomy things!" said the others. "Anything from floods to poisoned fish. Think of something cheerful!"

Then suddenly a great light appeared in the low place in the hills and the northern end of the lake turned golden. "The King beneath the Mountain!" they shouted. "His wealth is like the Sun, his silver like a fountain, his rivers golden run! The river is running gold from the Mountain!" they cried, and everywhere windows were opening and feet were hurrying.

There was once more a tremendous excitement and enthusiasm. But the grim-voiced fellow ran hotfoot to the Master. "The dragon is coming or I am a fool!" he cried. "Cut the bridges! To arms! To arms!"

Then warning trumpets were suddenly sounded, and echoed along the rocky shores. The cheering stopped and the joy was turned to dread. So it was that the dragon did not find them quite unprepared.

Before long, so great was his speed, they could see him as a spark of fire rushing towards them and growing ever huger and more bright, and not the most foolish doubted that the prophecies had gone rather wrong. Still they had a little time. Every vessel in the town was filled with water, every warrior was armed, every arrow and dart was ready, and the bridge to the land was thrown down and destroyed, before the roar of Smaug's terrible approach grew loud, and the lake rippled red as fire beneath the awful beating of his wings.

Amid shrieks and wailing and the shouts of men he came over them, swept towards the bridges and was foiled! The bridge was gone, and his enemies were on an island in deep water – too deep and dark and cool for his liking. If he plunged into it, a vapour and a steam would arise enough to cover all the land with a mist for days; but the lake was mightier than he, it would quench him before he could pass through.

Roaring, he swept back over the town. A hail of dark arrows leapt up and snapped and rattled on his scales and jewels, and their shafts fell back kindled by his breath burning and hissing into the lake. No fireworks you ever imagined equalled the sights that night. At the twanging of the bows and the shrilling of the trumpets the dragon's wrath blazed to its height, till he was blind and mad with it. No one had dared to give battle to him for many an age; nor would they have dared now, if it had not been for the grim-voiced man (Bard was his name), who ran to and fro cheering on the archers and urging the Master to order them to fight to the last arrow.

Fire leapt from the dragon's jaws. He circled for a while high in the air above them lighting all the lake; the trees by the shores shone like copper and like blood with leaping shadows of dense black at their feet. Then down he swooped straight through the arrow-storm, reckless in his rage, taking no heed to turn his scaly sides towards his foes, seeking only to set their town ablaze.

Fire leapt from thatched roofs and wooden beam-ends as he hurtled down and past and round again, though all had been drenched with water before he came. Once more water was flung by a hundred hands wherever a spark appeared. Back swirled the dragon. A sweep of his tail and the roof of the Great House crumbled and smashed down. Flames unquenchable sprang high into the night. Another swoop and another, and another house and then another sprang afire and fell; and still no arrow hindered Smaug or hurt him more than a fly from the marshes.

Already men were jumping into the water on every side. Women and children were being huddled into laden boats in the market-pool. Weapons were flung down. There was mourning and weeping, where but a little time ago the old songs of mirth to come had been sung about the dwarves. Now men cursed their names. The Master himself was turning to his great gilded boat, hoping to row away in the confusion and save himself. Soon all the town would be deserted and burnt down to the surface of the lake.

That was the dragon's hope. They could all get into boats

for all he cared. There he could have fine sport hunting them, or they could stop till they starved. Let them try to get to land and he would be ready. Soon he would set all the shoreland woods ablaze and wither every field and pasture. Just now he was enjoying the sport of town-baiting more than he had enjoyed anything for years.

But there was still a company of archers that held their ground among the burning houses. Their captain was Bard, grim-voiced and grim-faced, whose friends had accused him of prophesying floods and poisoned fish, though they knew his worth and courage. He was a descendant in long line of Girion, Lord of Dale, whose wife and child had escaped down the Running River from the ruin long ago. Now he shot with a great yew bow, till all his arrows but one were spent. The flames were near him. His companions were leaving him. He bent his bow for the last time.

Suddenly out of the dark something fluttered to his shoulder. He started – but it was only an old thrush. Unafraid it perched by his ear and it brought him news. Marvelling he found he could understand its tongue, for he was of the race of Dale.

"Wait! Wait!" it said to him. "The moon is rising. Look for the hollow of the left breast as he flies and turns above you!" And while Bard paused in wonder it told him of tidings up in the Mountain and of all that it had heard.

Then Bard drew his bow-string to his ear. The dragon was circling back, flying low, and as he came the moon rose above the eastern shore and silvered his great wings.

"Arrow!" said the bowman. "Black arrow! I have saved you to the last. You have never failed me and always I have recovered you. I had you from my father and he from old. If ever you came from the forges of the true King under the Mountain, go now and speed well!"

The dragon swooped once more lower than ever, and as he turned and dived down his belly glittered white with sparkling fires of gems in the moon – but not in one place. The great bow twanged. The black arrow sped straight from the string, straight for the hollow by the left breast where the foreleg was flung wide. In it smote and vanished, barb, shaft and feather, so fierce was its flight. With a shriek that deafened men, felled trees and split stone, Smaug shot spouting into the air, turned over and crashed down from on high in ruin.

Full on the town he fell. His last throes splintered it to sparks and gledes. The lake roared in. A vast steam leapt up, white in the sudden dark under the moon. There was a hiss, a gushing whirl, and then silence. And that was the end of Smaug and Esgaroth, but not of Bard.

The waxing moon rose higher and higher and the wind grew loud and cold. It twisted the white fog into bending pillars and hurrying clouds and drove it off to the West to scatter in tattered shreds over the marshes before Mirkwood. Then the many boats could be seen dotted dark on the surface of the lake, and down the wind came the voices of the people of Esgaroth lamenting their lost town and goods and ruined houses. But they had really much to be thankful for, had they thought of it, though it could hardly be expected that they should just then: three-quarters of the people of the town had at least escaped alive; their woods and fields and pastures and cattle and most of their boats remained undamaged; and the dragon was dead. What that meant they had not yet realized.

They gathered in mournful crowds upon the western shores, shivering in the cold wind, and their first complaints and anger were against the Master, who had left the town so soon, while some were still willing to defend it.

"He may have a good head for business – especially his own business," some murmured, "but he is no good when anything serious happens!" And they praised the courage of Bard and his last mighty shot. "If only he had not been killed," they all said, "we would make him a king. Bard the Dragon-shooter of the line of Girion! Alas that he is lost!"

And in the very midst of their talk a tall figure stepped from the shadows. He was drenched with water, his black hair hung wet over his face and shoulders, and a fierce light was in his eyes.

"Bard is not lost!" he cried. "He dived from Esgaroth, when the enemy was slain. I am Bard, of the line of Girion; I am the slayer of the dragon!"

"King Bard! King Bard!" they shouted; but the Master ground his chattering teeth.

"Girion was lord of Dale, not king of Esgaroth," he said. "In the Lake-town we have always elected masters from among the old and wise, and have not endured the rule of mere fighting men. Let 'King Bard' go back to his own kingdom – Dale is now freed by his valour, and nothing hinders his return. And any that wish can go with him, if they prefer the cold stones under the shadow of the Mountain to the green shores of the lake. The wise will stay here and hope to rebuild our town, and enjoy again in time its peace and riches."

"We will have King Bard!" the people near at hand shouted in reply. "We have had enough of the old men and the money-counters!" And people further off took up the cry: "Up the Bowman, and down with Moneybags," till the clamour echoed along the shore.

"I am the last man to undervalue Bard the Bowman," said the Master warily (for Bard now stood close beside him). "He has tonight earned an eminent place in the roll of the benefactors of our town; and he is worthy of many imperishable songs. But, why O People?" – and here the Master rose to his feet and spoke very loud and clear – "why do I get all your blame? For what fault am I to be deposed? Who aroused the dragon from his slumber, I might ask? Who obtained of us rich gifts and ample help, and led us to believe that old songs could come true? Who played on our soft hearts and our pleasant fancies? What sort of gold have they sent down the river to reward us? Dragon-fire and ruin! From whom should we claim the recompense of our damage, and aid for our widows and orphans?"

As you see, the Master had not got his position for nothing. The result of his words was that for the moment the people quite forgot their idea of a new king, and turned their angry thoughts towards Thorin and his company. Wild and bitter words were shouted from many sides; and some of those who had before sung the old songs loudest, were now heard as loudly crying that the dwarves had stirred the dragon up against them deliberately!

"Fools!" said Bard. "Why waste words and wrath on those unhappy creatures? Doubtless they perished first in fire, before Smaug came to us." Then even as he was speaking, the thought came into his heart of the fabled treasure of the Mountain lying without guard or owner, and he fell suddenly silent. He thought of the Master's words, and of Dale rebuilt, and filled with golden bells, if he could but find the men.

At length he spoke again: "This is no time for angry words, Master, or for considering weighty plans of change. There is work to do. I serve you still – though after a while I may think again of your words and go North with any that will follow me."

Then he strode off to help in the ordering of the camps and in the care of the sick and the wounded. But the Master scowled at his back as he went, and remained sitting on the ground. He thought much but said little, unless it was to call loudly for men to bring him fire and food.

Now everywhere Bard went he found talk running like fire among the people concerning the vast treasure that was now unguarded. Men spoke of the recompense for all their harm that they would soon get from it, and wealth over and to spare with which to buy things from the South; and it cheered them greatly in their plight. That was as well, for the night was bitter and miserable. Shelters could be contrived for few (the Master had one) and there was little food (even the Master went short). Many took ill of wet and cold and sorrow that night, and afterwards died, who had escaped uninjured from the ruin of the town; and in the days that followed there was much sickness and great hunger.

Meanwhile Bard took the lead, and ordered things as he wished, though always in the Master's name, and he had a hard task to govern the people and direct the preparations for their protection and housing. Probably most of them would have perished in the winter that now hurried after autumn, if help had not been to hand. But help came swiftly; for Bard at once had speedy messengers sent up the river to the Forest to ask the aid of the King of the Elves of the Wood, and these messengers had found a host already on the move, although it was then only the third day after the fall of Smaug.

The Elvenking had received news from his own messengers and from the birds that loved his folk, and already knew much of what had happened. Very great indeed was the commotion among all things with wings that dwelt on the borders of the Desolation of the Dragon. The air was filled with circling flocks, and their swift-flying messengers flew here and there across the sky. Above the borders of the Forest there was whistling, crying and piping. Far over Mirkwood tidings spread: "Smaug is dead!" Leaves rustled and startled ears were lifted. Even before the Elvenking rode forth the news had passed west right to the pine-woods of the Misty Mountains; Beorn had heard it in his wooden house, and the goblins were at council in their caves.

"That will be the last we shall hear of Thorin Oakenshield, I fear," said the king. "He would have done better to have remained my guest. It is an ill wind, all the same," he added, "that blows no one any good." For he too had not forgotten the legend of the wealth of Thror. So it was that Bard's messengers found him now marching with many spearmen and bowmen; and crows were gathered thick above him, for they thought that war was awakening again, such as had not been in those parts for a long age.

But the king, when he received the prayers of Bard, had pity, for he was the lord of a good and kindly people; so turning his march, which had at first been direct towards the Mountain, he hastened now down the river to the Long Lake. He had not boats or rafts enough for his host, and they were forced to go the slower way by foot; but great store of goods he sent ahead by water. Still elves are light-footed, and though they were not these days much used to the marshes and the treacherous lands between the Forest and the Lake, their going was swift. Only five days after the death of the dragon they came upon the shores and looked on the ruins of the town. Their welcome was good, as may be expected, and the men and their Master were ready to make any bargain for the future in return for the Elvenking's aid.

Their plans were soon made. With the women and the children, the old and the unfit, the Master remained behind; and with him were men of crafts and many skilled elves; and they busied themselves felling trees, and collecting the timber sent down from the Forest. Then they set about raising many huts by the shore against the oncoming winter; and also under the Master's direction they began the planning of a new town, designed more fair and large even than before, but not in the same place. They removed northward higher up the shore; for ever after they had a dread of the water where the dragon lay. He would never again return to his golden bed, but was stretched cold as stone, twisted upon the floor of the shallows. There for ages his huge bones could be seen in calm weather amid the ruined piles of the old town. But few dared to cross the cursed spot, and none dared to dive into the shivering water or recover the precious stones that fell from his rotting carcase.

But all the men of arms who were still able, and the most of the Elvenking's array, got ready to march north to the Mountain. It was thus that in eleven days from the ruin of the town the head of their host passed the rock-gates at the end of the lake and came into the desolate lands.

Chapter 15

The Gathering of the Clouds

Now we will return to Bilbo and the dwarves. All night one of them had watched, but when morning came they had not heard or seen any sign of danger. But ever more thickly the birds were gathering. The companies came flying from the South; and the crows that still lived about the Mountain were wheeling and crying unceasingly above.

"Something strange is happening," said Thorin. "The time has gone for the autumn wanderings; and these are birds that dwell always in the land; there are starlings and flocks of finches; and far off there are many carrion birds as if a battle were afoot!"

Suddenly Bilbo pointed: "There is that old thrush again!" he cried. "He seems to have escaped, when Smaug smashed the mountain-side, but I don't suppose the snails have!"

Sure enough the old thrush was there, and as Bilbo

pointed, he flew towards them and perched on a stone near by. Then he fluttered his wings and sang; then he cocked his head on one side, as if to listen; and again he sang, and again he listened.

"I believe he is trying to tell us something," said Balin; "but I cannot follow the speech of such birds, it is very quick and difficult. Can you make it out, Baggins?"

"Not very well," said Bilbo (as a matter of fact, he could make nothing of it at all); "but the old fellow seems very excited."

"I only wish he was a raven!" said Balin.

"I thought you did not like them! You seemed very shy of them, when we came this way before."

"Those were crows! And nasty suspicious-looking creatures at that, and rude as well. You must have heard the ugly names they were calling after us. But the ravens are different. There used to be great friendship between them and the people of Thror; and they often brought us secret news, and were rewarded with such bright things as they coveted to hide in their dwellings.

"They live many a year, and their memories are long, and they hand on their wisdom to their children. I knew many among the ravens of the rocks when I was a dwarf-lad. This very height was once named Ravenhill, because there was a wise and famous pair, old Carc and his wife, that lived here above the guard-chamber. But I don't suppose that any of that ancient breed linger here now."

No sooner had he finished speaking than the old thrush

gave a loud call, and immediately flew away.

"We may not understand him, but that old bird understands us, I am sure," said Balin. "Keep watch now, and see what happens!"

Before long there was a fluttering of wings, and back came the thrush; and with him came a most decrepit old bird. He was getting blind, he could hardly fly, and the top of his head was bald. He was an aged raven of great size. He alighted stiffly on the ground before them, slowly flapped his wings, and bobbed towards Thorin.

"O Thorin son of Thrain, and Balin son of Fundin," he croaked (and Bilbo could understand what he said, for he used ordinary language and not bird-speech). "I am Roäc son of Carc. Carc is dead, but he was well known to you once. It is a hundred years and three and fifty since I came out of the egg, but I do not forget what my father told me. Now I am the chief of the great ravens of the Mountain. We are few, but we remember still the old king that was of old. Most of my people are abroad, for there are great tidings in the South – some are tidings of joy to you, and some you will not think so good.

"Behold! the birds are gathering back again to the Mountain and to Dale from South and East and West, for word has gone out that Smaug is dead!"

"Dead! Dead?" shouted the dwarves. "Dead! Then we have been in needless fear – and the treasure is ours!" They all sprang up and began to caper about for joy.

"Yes, dead," said Roäc. "The thrush, may his feathers never

fall, saw him die, and we may trust his words. He saw him fall in battle with the men of Esgaroth the third night back from now at the rising of the moon."

It was some time before Thorin could bring the dwarves to be silent and listen to the raven's news. At length when he had told all the tale of the battle he went on:

"So much for joy, Thorin Oakenshield. You may go back to your halls in safety; all the treasure is yours – for the moment. But many are gathering hither beside the birds. The news of the death of the guardian has already gone far and wide, and the legend of the wealth of Thror has not lost in the telling during many years; many are eager for a share of the spoil. Already a host of the elves is on the way, and carrion birds are with them hoping for battle and slaughter. By the lake men murmur that their sorrows are due to the dwarves; for they are homeless and many have died, and Smaug has destroyed their town. They too think to find amends from your treasure, whether you are alive or dead.

"Your own wisdom must decide your course; but thirteen is small remnant of the great folk of Durin that once dwelt here, and now are scattered far. If you will listen to my counsel, you will not trust the Master of the Lake-men, but rather him that shot the dragon with his bow. Bard is he, of the race of Dale, of the line of Girion; he is a grim man but true. We would see peace once more among dwarves and men and elves after the long desolation; but it may cost you dear in gold. I have spoken."

Then Thorin burst forth in anger: "Our thanks, Roäc

Carc's son. You and your people shall not be forgotten. But none of our gold shall thieves take or the violent carry off while we are alive. If you would earn our thanks still more, bring us news of any that draw near. Also I would beg of you, if any of you are still young and strong of wing, that you would send messengers to our kin in the mountains of the North, both west from here and east, and tell them of our plight. But go specially to my cousin Dain in the Iron Hills, for he has many people well-armed, and dwells nearest to this place. Bid him hasten!"

"I will not say if this counsel be good or bad," croaked Roäc; "but I will do what can be done." Then off he slowly flew.

"Back now to the Mountain!" cried Thorin. "We have little time to lose."

"And little food to use!" cried Bilbo, always practical on such points. In any case he felt that the adventure was, properly speaking, over with the death of the dragon – in which he was much mistaken – and he would have given most of his share of the profits for the peaceful winding up of these affairs.

"Back to the Mountain!" cried the dwarves as if they had not heard him; so back he had to go with them.

As you have heard some of the events already, you will see that the dwarves still had some days before them. They explored the caverns once more, and found, as they expected, that only the Front Gate remained open; all the other gates (except, of course, the small secret door) had long ago been broken and blocked by Smaug, and no sign of them remained. So now they began to labour hard in fortifying the main entrance, and in making a new path that led from it. Tools were to be found in plenty that the miners and quarriers and builders of old had used; and at such work the dwarves were still very skilled.

As they worked the ravens brought them constant tidings. In this way they learnt that the Elvenking had turned aside to the Lake, and they still had a breathing space. Better still, they heard that three of their ponies had escaped and were wandering wild far down the banks of the Running River, not far from where the rest of their stores had been left. So while the others went on with their work, Fili and Kili were sent, guided by a raven, to find the ponies and bring back all they could.

They were four days gone, and by that time they knew that the joined armies of the Lake-men and the Elves were hurrying toward the Mountain. But now their hopes were higher, for they had food for some weeks with care – chiefly *cram*, of course, and they were very tired of it; but *cram* is much better than nothing – and already the gate was blocked with a wall of squared stones laid dry, but very thick and high, across the opening. There were holes in the wall through which they could see (or shoot), but no entrance. They climbed in or out with ladders, and hauled stuff up with ropes. For the issuing of the stream they had contrived a small low arch under the new wall; but near the entrance they had so altered the narrow bed that a wide pool stretched from the mountain-wall to the head of the fall over which the stream went towards Dale. Approach to the Gate was now only possible, without swimming, along a narrow ledge of the cliff, to the right as one looked outwards from the wall. The ponies they had brought only to the head of the steps above the old bridge, and unloading them there had bidden them return to their masters and sent them back riderless to the South.

There came a night when suddenly there were many lights as of fires and torches away south in Dale before them.

"They have come!" called Balin. "And their camp is very great. They must have come into the valley under the cover of dusk along both banks of the river."

That night the dwarves slept little. The morning was still pale when they saw a company approaching. From behind their wall they watched them come up to the valley's head and climb slowly up. Before long they could see that both men of the lake armed as if for war and elvish bowmen were among them. At length the foremost of these climbed the tumbled rocks and appeared at the top of the falls; and very great was their surprise to see the pool before them and the gate blocked with a wall of new-hewn stone.

As they stood pointing and speaking to one another Thorin hailed them: "Who are you," he called in a very loud voice, "that come as if in war to the gates of Thorin son of Thrain, King under the Mountain, and what do you desire?"

But they answered nothing. Some turned swiftly back,

and the others after gazing for a while at the Gate and its defences soon followed them. That day the camp was moved to the east of the river, right between the arms of the Mountain. The rocks echoed then with voices and with song, as they had not done for many a day. There was the sound, too, of elven-harps and of sweet music; and as it echoed up towards them it seemed that the chill of the air was warmed, and they caught faintly the fragrance of woodland flowers blossoming in spring.

Then Bilbo longed to escape from the dark fortress and to go down and join in the mirth and feasting by the fires. Some of the younger dwarves were moved in their hearts, too, and they muttered that they wished things had fallen out otherwise and that they might welcome such folk as friends; but Thorin scowled.

Then the dwarves themselves brought forth harps and instruments regained from the hoard, and made music to soften his mood; but their song was not an elvish song, and was much like the song they had sung long before in Bilbo's little hobbit-hole.

Under the Mountain dark and tall
The King has come unto his hall!
His foe is dead, the Worm of Dread,
And ever so his foes shall fall.

The sword is sharp, the spear is long,
The arrow swift, the Gate is strong;

The heart is bold that looks on gold;
The dwarves no more shall suffer wrong.

The dwarves of yore made mighty spells,
While hammers fell like ringing bells
In places deep, where dark things sleep,
In hollow halls beneath the fells.

On silver necklaces they strung
The light of stars, on crowns they hung
The dragon-fire, from twisted wire
The melody of harps they wrung.

The mountain throne once more is freed!
O! wandering folk, the summons heed!
Come haste! Come haste! across the waste!
The king of friend and kin has need.

Now call we over mountains cold,
"Come back unto the caverns old!"
Here at the Gates the king awaits,
His hands are rich with gems and gold.

The king is come unto his hall
Under the Mountain dark and tall.
The Worm of Dread is slain and dead,
And ever so our foes shall fall!

This song appeared to please Thorin, and he smiled again and grew merry; and he began reckoning the distance to the Iron Hills and how long it would be before Dain could reach the Lonely Mountain, if he had set out as soon as the message reached him. But Bilbo's heart fell, both at the song and the talk: they sounded much too warlike.

The next morning early a company of spearmen was seen crossing the river, and marching up the valley. They bore with them the green banner of the Elvenking and the blue banner of the Lake, and they advanced until they stood right before the wall at the Gate.

Again Thorin hailed them in a loud voice: "Who are you that come armed for war to the gates of Thorin son of Thrain, King under the Mountain?" This time he was answered.

A tall man stood forward, dark of hair and grim of face, and he cried: "Hail Thorin! Why do you fence yourself like a robber in his hold? We are not yet foes, and we rejoice that you are alive beyond our hope. We came expecting to find none living here; yet now that we are met there is matter for a parley and a council."

"Who are you, and of what would you parley?"

"I am Bard, and by my hand was the dragon slain and your treasure delivered. Is that not a matter that concerns you? Moreover I am by right descent the heir of Girion of Dale, and in your hoard is mingled much of the wealth of his halls and towns, which old Smaug stole. Is not that a matter of which we may speak? Further in his last battle

Smaug destroyed the dwellings of the men of Esgaroth, and I am yet the servant of their Master. I would speak for him and ask whether you have no thought for the sorrow and misery of his people. They aided you in your distress, and in recompense you have thus far brought ruin only, though doubtless undesigned."

Now these were fair words and true, if proudly and grimly spoken; and Bilbo thought that Thorin would at once admit what justice was in them. He did not, of course, expect that any one would remember that it was he who discovered all by himself the dragon's weak spot; and that was just as well, for no one ever did. But also he did not reckon with the power that gold has upon which a dragon has long brooded, nor with dwarvish hearts. Long hours in the past days Thorin had spent in the treasury, and the lust of it was heavy on him. Though he had hunted chiefly for the Arkenstone, yet he had an eye for many another wonderful thing that was lying there, about which were wound old memories of the labours and the sorrows of his race.

"You put your worst cause last and in the chief place," Thorin answered. "To the treasure of my people no man has a claim, because Smaug who stole it from us also robbed him of life or home. The treasure was not his that his evil deeds should be amended with a share of it. The price of the goods and the assistance that we received of the Lake-men we will fairly pay – in due time. But *nothing* will we give, not even a loaf's worth, under threat of force. While an armed host lies before our doors, we look on you as foes and thieves.

"It is in my mind to ask what share of their inheritance you would have paid to our kindred, had you found the hoard unguarded and us slain."

"A just question," replied Bard. "But you are not dead, and we are not robbers. Moreover the wealthy may have pity beyond right on the needy that befriended them when they were in want. And still my other claims remain unanswered."

"I will not parley, as I have said, with armed men at my gate. Nor at all with the people of the Elvenking, whom I remember with small kindness. In this debate they have no place. Begone now ere our arrows fly! And if you would speak with me again, first dismiss the elvish host to the woods where it belongs, and then return, laying down your arms before you approach the threshold."

"The Elvenking is my friend, and he has succoured the people of the Lake in their need, though they had no claim but friendship on him," answered Bard. "We will give you time to repent your words. Gather your wisdom ere we return!" Then he departed and went back to the camp.

Ere many hours were past, the banner-bearers returned, and trumpeters stood forth and blew a blast:

"In the name of Esgaroth and the Forest," one cried, "we speak unto Thorin Thrain's son Oakenshield, calling himself the King under the Mountain, and we bid him consider well the claims that have been urged, or be declared our foe. At the least he shall deliver one twelfth portion of the treasure unto Bard, as the dragon-slayer, and as the heir of Girion. From that portion Bard will himself contribute to the aid of

Esgaroth; but if Thorin would have the friendship and honour of the lands about, as his sires had of old, then he will give also somewhat of his own for the comfort of the men of the Lake."

Then Thorin seized a bow of horn and shot an arrow at the speaker. It smote into his shield and stuck there quivering.

"Since such is your answer," he called in return, "I declare the Mountain besieged. You shall not depart from it, until you call on your side for a truce and a parley. We will bear no weapons against you, but we leave you to your gold. You may eat that, if you will!"

With that the messengers departed swiftly, and the dwarves were left to consider their case. So grim had Thorin become, that even if they had wished, the others would not have dared to find fault with him; but indeed most of them seemed to share his mind – except perhaps old fat Bombur and Fili and Kili. Bilbo, of course, disapproved of the whole turn of affairs. He had by now had more than enough of the Mountain, and being besieged inside it was not at all to his taste.

"The whole place still stinks of dragon," he grumbled to himself, "and it makes me sick. And *cram* is beginning simply to stick in my throat."

Chapter 16

A Thief in the Night

Now the days passed slowly and wearily. Many of the dwarves spent their time piling and ordering the treasure; and Thorin spoke of the Arkenstone of Thrain, and bade them eagerly to look for it in every corner.

"For the Arkenstone of my father," he said, "is worth more than a river of gold itself, and to me it is beyond price. That stone of all the treasure I name unto myself, and I will be avenged on anyone who finds it and withholds it."

Bilbo heard these words and he grew afraid, wondering what would happen, if the stone was found – wrapped in an old bundle of tattered oddments that he used as a pillow. All the same he did not speak of it, for as the weariness of the days grew heavier, the beginnings of a plan had come into his little head.

Things had gone on like this for some time, when the

ravens brought news that Dain and more than five hundred dwarves, hurrying from the Iron Hills, were now within about two days' march of Dale, coming from the north-east.

"But they cannot reach the Mountain unmarked," said Roäc, "and I fear lest there be battle in the valley. I do not call this counsel good. Though they are a grim folk, they are not likely to overcome the host that besets you; and even if they did so, what will you gain? Winter and snow is hastening behind them. How shall you be fed without the friendship and goodwill of the lands about you? The treasure is likely to be your death, though the dragon is no more!"

But Thorin was not moved. "Winter and snow will bite both men and elves," he said, "and they may find their dwellings in the waste grievous to bear. With my friends behind them and winter upon them, they will perhaps be in softer mood to parley with."

That night Bilbo made up his mind. The sky was black and moonless. As soon as it was full dark, he went to a corner of an inner chamber just within the gate and drew from his bundle a rope, and also the Arkenstone wrapped in a rag. Then he climbed to the top of the wall. Only Bombur was there, for it was his turn to watch, and the dwarves kept only one watchman at a time.

"It is mighty cold!" said Bombur. "I wish we could have a fire up here as they have in the camp!"

"It is warm enough inside," said Bilbo.

"I daresay; but I am bound here till midnight," grumbled the fat dwarf. "A sorry business altogether. Not that I venture to disagree with Thorin, may his beard grow ever longer; yet he was ever a dwarf with a stiff neck."

"Not as stiff as my legs," said Bilbo. "I am tired of stairs and stone passages. I would give a good deal for the feel of grass at my toes."

"I would give a good deal for the feel of a strong drink in my throat, and for a soft bed after a good supper!"

"I can't give you those, while the siege is going on. But it is long since I watched, and I will take your turn for you, if you like. There is no sleep in me tonight."

"You are a good fellow, Mr Baggins, and I will take your offer kindly. If there should be anything to note, rouse me first, mind you! I will lie in the inner chamber to the left, not far away."

"Off you go!" said Bilbo. "I will wake you at midnight, and you can wake the next watchman."

As soon as Bombur had gone, Bilbo put on his ring, fastened his rope, slipped down over the wall, and was gone. He had about five hours before him. Bombur would sleep (he could sleep at any time, and ever since the adventure in the forest he was always trying to recapture the beautiful dreams he had then); and all the others were busy with Thorin. It was unlikely that any, even Fili or Kili, would come out on the wall until it was their turn.

It was very dark, and the road after a while, when he left the newly made path and climbed down towards the lower course of the stream, was strange to him. At last he came to the bend where he had to cross the water, if he was to make for the camp, as he wished. The bed of the stream was there shallow but already broad, and fording it in the dark was not easy for the little hobbit. He was nearly across when he missed his footing on a round stone and fell into the cold water with a splash. He had barely scrambled out on the far bank, shivering and spluttering, when up came elves in the gloom with bright lanterns and searched for the cause of the noise.

"That was no fish!" one said. "There is a spy about. Hide your lights! They will help him more than us, if it is that queer little creature that is said to be their servant."

"Servant, indeed!" snorted Bilbo; and in the middle of his snort he sneezed loudly, and the elves immediately gathered towards the sound.

"Let's have a light!" he said. "I am here, if you want me!" and he slipped off his ring, and popped from behind a rock.

They seized him quickly, in spite of their surprise. "Who are you? Are you the dwarves' hobbit? What are you doing? How did you get so far past our sentinels?" they asked one after another.

"I am Mr Bilbo Baggins," he answered, "companion of Thorin, if you want to know. I know your king well by sight, though perhaps he doesn't know me to look at. But Bard will remember me, and it is Bard I particularly want to see."

"Indeed!" said they, "and what may be your business?"

"Whatever it is, it's my own, my good elves. But if you wish ever to get back to your own woods from this cold cheerless place," he answered shivering, "you will take me along quick to a fire, where I can dry – and then you will let me speak to your chiefs as quick as may be. I have only an hour or two to spare."

That is how it came about that some two hours after his escape from the Gate, Bilbo was sitting beside a warm fire in front of a large tent, and there sat too, gazing curiously at him, both the Elvenking and Bard. A hobbit in elvish armour, partly wrapped in an old blanket, was something new to them.

"Really you know," Bilbo was saying in his best business manner, "things are impossible. Personally I am tired of the whole affair. I wish I was back in the West in my own home, where folk are more reasonable. But I have an interest in this matter – one fourteenth share, to be precise, according to a letter, which fortunately I believe I have kept." He drew from a pocket in his old jacket (which he still wore over his mail), crumpled and much folded, Thorin's letter that had been put under the clock on his mantelpiece in May!

"A share in the *profits*, mind you," he went on. "I am aware of that. Personally I am only too ready to consider all your claims carefully, and deduct what is right from the total before putting in my own claim. However you don't know Thorin Oakenshield as well as I do now. I assure you, he is quite ready to sit on a heap of gold and starve, as long as you sit here."

"Well, let him!" said Bard. "Such a fool deserves to starve."

"Quite so," said Bilbo. "I see your point of view. At the same time winter is coming on fast. Before long you will be having snow and what not, and supplies will be difficult – even for elves I imagine. Also there will be other difficulties. You have not heard of Dain and the dwarves of the Iron Hills?"

"We have, a long time ago; but what has he got to do with us?" asked the king.

"I thought as much. I see I have some information you have not got. Dain, I may tell you, is now less than two days' march off, and has at least five hundred grim dwarves with him – a good many of them have had experience in the dreadful dwarf and goblin wars, of which you have no doubt heard. When they arrive there may be serious trouble."

"Why do you tell us this? Are you betraying your friends, or are you threatening us?" asked Bard grimly.

"My dear Bard!" squeaked Bilbo. "Don't be so hasty! I never met such suspicious folk! I am merely trying to avoid trouble for all concerned. Now I will make you an offer!"

"Let us hear it!" they said.

"You may see it!" said he. "It is this!" and he drew forth the Arkenstone, and threw away the wrapping.

The Elvenking himself, whose eyes were used to things of wonder and beauty, stood up in amazement. Even Bard gazed marvelling at it in silence. It was as if a globe had been filled with moonlight and hung before them in a net woven of the glint of frosty stars.

"This is the Arkenstone of Thrain," said Bilbo, "the Heart of the Mountain; and it is also the heart of Thorin. He values it above a river of gold. I give it to you. It will aid you in your bargaining." Then Bilbo, not without a shudder, not without a glance of longing, handed the marvellous stone to Bard, and he held it in his hand, as though dazed.

"But how is it yours to give?" he asked at last with an effort.

"O well!" said the hobbit uncomfortably. "It isn't exactly; but, well, I am willing to let it stand against all my claim, don't you know. I may be a burglar – or so they say: personally I never really felt like one – but I am an honest one, I hope, more or less. Anyway I am going back now, and the dwarves can do what they like to me. I hope you will find it useful."

The Elvenking looked at Bilbo with a new wonder. "Bilbo Baggins!" he said. "You are more worthy to wear the armour of elf-princes than many that have looked more comely in it. But I wonder if Thorin Oakenshield will see it so. I have more knowledge of dwarves in general than you have perhaps. I advise you to remain with us, and here you shall be honoured and thrice welcome."

"Thank you very much I am sure," said Bilbo with a bow. "But I don't think I ought to leave my friends like this, after all we have gone through together. And I promised to wake old Bombur at midnight, too! Really I must be going, and quickly."

Nothing they could say would stop him; so an escort was provided for him, and as he went both the king and Bard saluted him with honour. As they passed through the camp an old man, wrapped in a dark cloak, rose from a tent door where he was sitting and came towards them.

"Well done! Mr Baggins!" he said, clapping Bilbo on the back. "There is always more about you than anyone expects!" It was Gandalf.

For the first time for many a day Bilbo was really delighted. But there was no time for all the questions that he immediately wished to ask.

"All in good time!" said Gandalf. "Things are drawing towards the end now, unless I am mistaken. There is an unpleasant time just in front of you; but keep your heart up! You *may* come through all right. There is news brewing that even the ravens have not heard. Good night!"

Puzzled but cheered, Bilbo hurried on. He was guided to a safe ford and set across dry, and then he said farewell to the elves and climbed carefully back towards the Gate. Great weariness began to come over him; but it was well before midnight when he clambered up the rope again – it was still where he had left it. He untied it and hid it, and then he sat down on the wall and wondered anxiously what would happen next.

At midnight he woke up Bombur; and then in turn rolled himself up in his corner, without listening to the old dwarf's thanks (which he felt he had hardly earned). He was soon fast asleep forgetting all his worries till the morning. As a matter of fact he was dreaming of eggs and bacon.

Chapter 17

THE CLOUDS BURST

NEXT DAY THE trumpets rang early in the camp. Soon a single runner was seen hurrying along the narrow path. At a distance he stood and hailed them, asking whether Thorin would now listen to another embassy, since new tidings had come to hand, and matters were changed.

"That will be Dain!" said Thorin when he heard. "They will have got wind of his coming. I thought that would alter their mood! Bid them come few in number and weaponless, and I will hear," he called to the messenger.

About midday the banners of the Forest and the Lake were seen to be borne forth again. A company of twenty was approaching. At the beginning of the narrow way they laid aside sword and spear, and came on towards the Gate. Wondering, the dwarves saw that among them were both Bard and the Elvenking, before whom an old man wrapped in cloak and hood bore a strong casket of iron-bound wood.

"Hail Thorin!" said Bard. "Are you still of the same mind?"

"My mind does not change with the rising and setting of a few suns," answered Thorin. "Did you come to ask me idle questions? Still the elf-host has not departed as I bade! Till then you come in vain to bargain with me."

"Is there then nothing for which you would yield any of your gold?"

"Nothing that you or your friends have to offer."

"What of the Arkenstone of Thrain?" said he, and at the same moment the old man opened the casket and held aloft the jewel. The light leapt from his hand, bright and white in the morning.

Then Thorin was stricken dumb with amazement and confusion. No one spoke for a long while.

Thorin at length broke the silence, and his voice was thick with wrath. "That stone was my father's, and is mine," he said. "Why should I purchase my own?" But wonder overcame him and he added: "But how came you by the heirloom of my house – if there is need to ask such a question of thieves?"

"We are not thieves," Bard answered. "Your own we will give back in return for our own."

"How came you by it?" shouted Thorin in gathering rage.

"I gave it them!" squeaked Bilbo, who was peeping over the wall, by now in a dreadful fright.

"You! You!" cried Thorin, turning upon him and grasping him with both hands. "You miserable hobbit! You undersized

– burglar!" he shouted at a loss for words, and he shook poor Bilbo like a rabbit.

"By the beard of Durin! I wish I had Gandalf here! Curse him for his choice of you! May his beard wither! As for you I will throw you to the rocks!" he cried and lifted Bilbo in his arms.

"Stay! Your wish is granted!" said a voice. The old man with the casket threw aside his hood and cloak. "Here is Gandalf! And none too soon it seems. If you don't like my Burglar, please don't damage him. Put him down, and listen first to what he has to say!"

"You all seem in league!" said Thorin dropping Bilbo on the top of the wall. "Never again will I have dealings with any wizard or his friends. What have you to say, you descendant of rats?"

"Dear me! Dear me!" said Bilbo. "I am sure this is all very uncomfortable. You may remember saying that I might choose my own fourteenth share! Perhaps I took it too literally – I have been told that dwarves are sometimes politer in word than in deed. The time was, all the same, when you seemed to think that I had been of some service. Descendant of rats, indeed! Is this all the service of you and your family that I was promised, Thorin? Take it that I have disposed of my share as I wished, and let it go at that!"

"I will," said Thorin grimly. "And I will let you go at that – and may we never meet again!" Then he turned and spoke over the wall. "I am betrayed," he said. "It was rightly guessed that I could not forbear to redeem the Arkenstone, the treasure of my house. For it I will give one fourteenth share of the hoard in silver and gold, setting aside the gems; but that shall be accounted the promised share of this traitor, and with that reward he shall depart, and you can divide it as you will. He will get little enough, I doubt not. Take him, if you wish him to live; and no friendship of mine goes with him.

"Get down now to your friends!" he said to Bilbo, "or I will throw you down."

"What about the gold and silver?" asked Bilbo.

"That shall follow after, as can be arranged," said he. "Get down!"

"Until then we keep the stone," cried Bard.

"You are not making a very splendid figure as King under the Mountain," said Gandalf. "But things may change yet."

"They may indeed," said Thorin. And already, so strong was the bewilderment of the treasure upon him, he was pondering whether by the help of Dain he might not recapture the Arkenstone and withhold the share of the reward.

And so Bilbo was swung down from the wall, and departed with nothing for all his trouble, except the armour which Thorin had given him already. More than one of the dwarves in their hearts felt shame and pity at his going.

"Farewell!" he cried to them. "We may meet again as friends."

"Be off!" cried Thorin. "You have mail upon you, which was made by my folk, and is too good for you. It cannot be pierced by arrows; but if you do not hasten, I will sting your miserable feet. So be swift!"

"Not so hasty!" said Bard. "We will give you until tomorrow. At noon we will return, and see if you have brought from the hoard the portion that is to be set against the stone. If that is done without deceit, then we will depart, and the elf-host will go back to the Forest. In the meanwhile farewell!"

With that they went back to the camp; but Thorin sent messengers by Roäc telling Dain of what had passed, and bidding him come with wary speed.

That day passed and the night. The next day the wind shifted west, and the air was dark and gloomy. The morning was still early when a cry was heard in the camp. Runners came in to report that a host of dwarves had appeared round the eastern spur of the Mountain and was now hastening to Dale. Dain had come. He had hurried on through the night, and so had come upon them sooner than they had expected. Each one of his folk was clad in a hauberk of steel mail that hung to his knees, and his legs were covered with hose of a fine and flexible metal mesh, the secret of whose making was possessed by Dain's people. The dwarves are exceedingly strong for their height, but most of these were strong even for dwarves. In battle they wielded heavy two-handed mattocks; but each of them had also a short broad sword at his side and a round-shield slung at his back. Their beards were forked and plaited and thrust into their belts. Their caps were of iron and they were shod with iron, and their faces were grim.

Trumpets called men and elves to arms. Before long the

dwarves could be seen coming up the valley at a great pace. They halted between the river and the eastern spur; but a few held on their way, and crossing the river drew near the camp; and there they laid down their weapons and held up their hands in sign of peace. Bard went out to meet them, and with him went Bilbo.

"We are sent from Dain son of Nain," they said when questioned. "We are hastening to our kinsmen in the Mountain, since we learn that the kingdom of old is renewed. But who are you that sit in the plain as foes before defended walls?" This, of course, in the polite and rather old-fashioned language of such occasions, meant simply: "You have no business here. We are going on, so make way or we shall fight you!" They meant to push on between the Mountain and the loop of the river; for the narrow land there did not seem to be strongly guarded.

Bard, of course, refused to allow the dwarves to go straight on to the Mountain. He was determined to wait until the gold and silver had been brought out in exchange for the Arkenstone; for he did not believe that this would be done, if once the fortress was manned with so large and warlike a company. They had brought with them a great store of supplies; for the dwarves can carry very heavy burdens, and nearly all of Dain's folk, in spite of their rapid march, bore huge packs on their backs in addition to their weapons. They would stand a siege for weeks, and by the time yet more dwarves might come, and yet more, for Thorin had many relatives. Also they would be able to reopen and guard some other gate, so that the besiegers would have to encircle the whole mountain; and for that they had not sufficient numbers.

These were, in fact, precisely their plans (for the raven-messengers had been busy between Thorin and Dain); but for the moment the way was barred, so after angry words the dwarf-messengers retired muttering in their beards. Bard then sent messengers at once to the Gate; but they found no gold or payment. Arrows came forth as soon as they were within shot, and they hastened back in dismay. In the camp all was now astir, as if for battle; for the dwarves of Dain were advancing along the eastern bank.

"Fools!" laughed Bard, "to come thus beneath the Mountain's arm! They do not understand war above ground, whatever they may know of battle in the mines. There are many of our archers and spearmen now hidden in the rocks upon their right flank. Dwarf-mail may be good, but they will soon be hard put to it. Let us set on them now from both sides, before they are fully rested!"

But the Elvenking said: "Long will I tarry, ere I begin this war for gold. The dwarves cannot pass us, unless we will, or do anything that we cannot mark. Let us hope still for something that will bring reconciliation. Our advantage in numbers will be enough, if in the end it must come to unhappy blows."

But he reckoned without the dwarves. The knowledge that the Arkenstone was in the hands of the besiegers burnt in their thoughts; also they guessed the hesitation of Bard and his friends, and resolved to strike while they debated.

Suddenly without a signal they sprang silently forward to attack. Bows twanged and arrows whistled; battle was about to be joined.

Still more suddenly a darkness came on with dreadful swiftness! A black cloud hurried over the sky. Winter thunder on a wild wind rolled roaring up and rumbled in the Mountain, and lightning lit its peak. And beneath the thunder another blackness could be seen whirling forward; but it did not come with the wind, it came from the North, like a vast cloud of birds, so dense that no light could be seen between their wings.

"Halt!" cried Gandalf, who appeared suddenly, and stood alone, with arms uplifted, between the advancing dwarves and the ranks awaiting them. "Halt!" he called in a voice like thunder, and his staff blazed forth with a flash like the lightning. "Dread has come upon you all! Alas! it has come more swiftly than I guessed. The Goblins are upon you! Bolg* of the North is coming, O Dain! whose father you slew in Moria. Behold! the bats are above his army like a sea of locusts. They ride upon wolves and Wargs are in their train!"

Amazement and confusion fell upon them all. Even as Gandalf had been speaking the darkness grew. The dwarves halted and gazed at the sky. The elves cried out with many voices.

"Come!" called Gandalf. "There is yet time for council. Let Dain son of Nain come swiftly to us!"

*Son of Azog. See p.40

★ ★ ★

So began a battle that none had expected; and it was called the Battle of Five Armies, and it was very terrible. Upon one side were the Goblins and the wild Wolves, and upon the other were Elves and Men and Dwarves. This is how it fell out. Ever since the fall of the Great Goblin of the Misty Mountains the hatred of their race for the dwarves had been rekindled to fury. Messengers had passed to and fro between all their cities, colonies and strongholds; for they resolved now to win the dominion of the North. Tidings they had gathered in secret ways; and in all the mountains there was a forging and an arming. Then they marched and gathered by hill and valley, going ever by tunnel or under dark, until around and beneath the great mountain Gundabad of the North, where was their capital, a vast host was assembled ready to sweep down in time of storm unawares upon the South. Then they learnt of the death of Smaug, and joy was in their hearts; and they hastened night after night through the mountains, and came thus at last on a sudden from the North hard on the heels of Dain. Not even the ravens knew of their coming until they came out in the broken lands which divided the Lonely Mountain from the hills behind. How much Gandalf knew cannot be said, but it is plain that he had not expected this sudden assault.

This is the plan that he made in council with the Elvenking and with Bard; and with Dain, for the dwarf-lord now joined them: the goblins were the foes of all, and at their coming all other quarrels were forgotten. Their only hope was to lure the goblins into the valley between the arms of the Mountain; and themselves to man the great spurs that struck south and east. Yet this would be perilous, if the goblins were in sufficient numbers to overrun the Mountain itself, and so attack them also from behind and above; but there was no time to make any other plan, or to summon any help.

Soon the thunder passed, rolling away to the south-east; but the bat-cloud came, flying lower, over the shoulder of the Mountain, and whirled above them shutting out the light and filling them with dread.

"To the Mountain!" called Bard. "To the Mountain! Let us take our places while there is yet time!"

On the southern spur, in its lower slopes and in the rocks at its feet, the Elves were set; on the eastern spur were men and dwarves. But Bard and some of the nimblest of men and elves climbed to the height of the eastern shoulder to gain a view to the north. Soon they could see the lands before the Mountain's feet black with a hurrying multitude. Ere long the vanguard swirled round the spur's end and came rushing into Dale. These were the swiftest wolf-riders, and already their cries and howls rent the air afar. A few brave men were strung before them to make a feint of resistance, and many there fell before the rest drew back and fled to either side. As Gandalf had hoped, the goblin army had gathered behind the resisted vanguard, and poured now in rage into the valley, driving wildly up between the arms of the Mountain, seeking for the foe. Their banners were countless, black and red, and they came on like a tide in fury and disorder.

It was a terrible battle. The most dreadful of all Bilbo's experiences, and the one which at the time he hated most – which is to say it was the one he was most proud of, and most fond of recalling long afterwards, although he was quite unimportant in it. Actually I may say he put on his ring early in the business and vanished from sight, if not from all danger. A magic ring of that sort is not a complete protection in a goblin charge, nor does it stop flying arrows and wild spears; but it does help in getting out of the way, and it prevents your head from being specially chosen for a sweeping stroke by a goblin swordsman.

The elves were the first to charge. Their hatred for the goblins is cold and bitter. Their spears and swords shone in the gloom with a gleam of chill flame, so deadly was the wrath of the hands that held them. As soon as the host of their enemies was dense in the valley, they sent against it a shower of arrows, and each flickered as it fled as if with stinging fire. Behind the arrows a thousand of their spearmen leapt down and charged. The yells were deafening. The rocks were stained black with goblin blood.

Just as the goblins were recovering from the onslaught and the elf-charge was halted, there rose from across the valley a deep-throated roar. With cries of "Moria!" and "Dain, Dain!" the dwarves of the Iron Hills plunged in, wielding their mattocks, upon the other side; and beside them came the men of the Lake with long swords.

Panic came upon the goblins; and even as they turned to meet this new attack, the elves charged again with renewed numbers. Already many of the goblins were flying back down the river to escape from the trap; and many of their own wolves were turning upon them and rending the dead and the wounded. Victory seemed at hand, when a cry rang out on the heights above.

Goblins had scaled the Mountain from the other side and already many were on the slopes above the Gate, and others were streaming down recklessly, heedless of those that fell screaming from cliff and precipice, to attack the spurs from above. Each of these could be reached by paths that ran down from the main mass of the Mountain in the centre; and the defenders had too few to bar the way for long. Victory now vanished from hope. They had only stemmed the first onslaught of the black tide.

Day drew on. The goblins gathered again in the valley. There a host of Wargs came ravening and with them came the bodyguard of Bolg, goblins of huge size with scimitars of steel. Soon actual darkness was coming into a stormy sky; while still the great bats swirled about the heads and ears of elves and men, or fastened vampire-like on the stricken. Now Bard was fighting to defend the eastern spur, and yet giving slowly back; and the elf-lords were at bay about their king upon the southern arm, near to the watch-post on Ravenhill.

Suddenly there was a great shout, and from the Gate came a trumpet call. They had forgotten Thorin! Part of the wall, moved by levers, fell outward with a crash into the pool. Out leapt the King under the Mountain, and his companions followed him. Hood and cloak were gone; they were in shining armour, and red light leapt from their eyes. In the gloom the great dwarf gleamed like gold in a dying fire.

Rocks were hurled down from on high by the goblins above; but they held on, leapt down to the falls' foot, and rushed forward to battle. Wolf and rider fell or fled before them. Thorin wielded his axe with mighty strokes, and nothing seemed to harm him.

"To me! To me! Elves and Men! To me! O my kinsfolk!" he cried, and his voice shook like a horn in the valley.

Down, heedless of order, rushed all the dwarves of Dain to his help. Down too came many of the Lake-men, for Bard could not restrain them; and out upon the other side came many of the spearmen of the elves. Once again the goblins were stricken in the valley; and they were piled in heaps till Dale was dark and hideous with their corpses. The Wargs were scattered and Thorin drove right against the bodyguard of Bolg. But he could not pierce their ranks.

Already behind him among the goblin dead lay many men and many dwarves, and many a fair elf that should have lived yet long ages merrily in the wood. And as the valley widened his onset grew ever slower. His numbers were too few. His flanks were unguarded. Soon the attackers were attacked, and they were forced into a great ring, facing every way, hemmed all about with goblins and wolves returning to the assault. The bodyguard of Bolg came howling against them, and drove in upon their ranks like waves upon cliffs of sand. Their friends could not help them, for the assault from the Mountain was renewed with redoubled force, and upon either side men and elves were being slowly beaten down.

On all this Bilbo looked with misery. He had taken his stand on Ravenhill among the Elves – partly because there was more chance of escape from that point, and partly (with the more Tookish part of his mind) because if he was going to be in a last desperate stand, he preferred on the whole to defend the Elvenking. Gandalf, too, I may say, was there, sitting on the ground as if in deep thought, preparing, I suppose, some last blast of magic before the end.

That did not seem far off. "It will not be long now," thought Bilbo, "before the goblins win the Gate, and we are all slaughtered or driven down and captured. Really it is enough to make one weep, after all one has gone through. I would rather old Smaug had been left with all the wretched treasure, than that these vile creatures should get it, and poor old Bombur, and Balin and Fili and Kili and all the rest come to a bad end; and Bard too, and the Lake-men and the merry elves. Misery me! I have heard songs of many battles, and I have always understood that defeat may be glorious. It seems very uncomfortable, not to say distressing. I wish I was well out of it."

The clouds were torn by the wind, and a red sunset slashed the West. Seeing the sudden gleam in the gloom Bilbo looked round. He gave a great cry: he had seen a sight that made his heart leap, dark shapes small yet majestic against the distant glow.

"The Eagles! The Eagles!" he shouted. "The Eagles are coming!"

Bilbo's eyes were seldom wrong. The eagles were coming down the wind, line after line, in such a host as must have gathered from all the eyries of the North.

"The Eagles! The Eagles!" Bilbo cried, dancing and waving his arms. If the elves could not see him they could hear him. Soon they too took up the cry, and it echoed across the valley. Many wondering eyes looked up, though as yet nothing could be seen except from the southern shoulders of the Mountain.

"The Eagles!" cried Bilbo once more, but at that moment a stone hurtling from above smote heavily on his helm, and he fell with a crash and knew no more.

Chapter 18

THE RETURN JOURNEY

WHEN BILBO CAME to himself, he was literally by himself. He was lying on the flat stones of Ravenhill, and no one was near. A cloudless day, but cold, was broad above him. He was shaking, and as chilled as stone, but his head burnt with fire.

"Now I wonder what has happened?" he said to himself. "At any rate I am not yet one of the fallen heroes; but I suppose there is still time enough for that!"

He sat up painfully. Looking into the valley he could see no living goblins. After a while his head cleared a little, he thought he could see elves moving in the rocks below. He rubbed his eyes. Surely there was a camp still in the plain some distance off; and there was a coming and going about the Gate? Dwarves seemed to be busy removing the wall. But all was deadly still. There was no call and no echo of a song. Sorrow seemed to be in the air.

"Victory after all, I suppose!" he said, feeling his aching head. "Well, it seems a very gloomy business."

Suddenly he was aware of a man climbing up and coming towards him.

"Hullo there!" he called with a shaky voice. "Hullo there! What news?"

"What voice is it that speaks among the stones?" said the man halting and peering about him not far from where Bilbo sat.

Then Bilbo remembered his ring! "Well I'm blessed!" said he. "This invisibility has its drawbacks after all. Otherwise I suppose I might have spent a warm and comfortable night in bed!"

"It's me, Bilbo Baggins, companion of Thorin!" he cried, hurriedly taking off the ring.

"It is well that I have found you!" said the man striding forward. "You are needed and we have looked for you long. You would have been numbered among the dead, who are many, if Gandalf the wizard had not said that your voice was last heard in this place. I have been sent to look here for the last time. Are you much hurt?"

"A nasty knock on the head, I think," said Bilbo. "But I have a helm and a hard skull. All the same I feel sick and my legs are like straws."

"I will carry you down to the camp in the valley," said the man, and picked him lightly up.

The man was swift and sure-footed. It was not long before Bilbo was set down before a tent in Dale; and there stood

Gandalf, with his arm in a sling. Even the wizard had not escaped without a wound; and there were few unharmed in all the host.

When Gandalf saw Bilbo, he was delighted. "Baggins!" he exclaimed. "Well I never! Alive after all – I *am* glad! I began to wonder if even your luck would see you through! A terrible business, and it nearly was disastrous. But other news can wait. Come!" he said more gravely. "You are called for"; and leading the hobbit he took him within the tent.

"Hail, Thorin!" he said as he entered. "I have brought him."

There indeed lay Thorin Oakenshield, wounded with many wounds, and his rent armour and notched axe were cast upon the floor. He looked up as Bilbo came beside him.

"Farewell, good thief," he said. "I go now to the halls of waiting to sit beside my fathers, until the world is renewed. Since I leave now all gold and silver, and go where it is of little worth, I wish to part in friendship from you, and I would take back my words and deeds at the Gate."

Bilbo knelt on one knee filled with sorrow. "Farewell, King under the Mountain!" he said. "This is a bitter adventure, if it must end so; and not a mountain of gold can amend it. Yet I am glad that I have shared in your perils – that has been more than any Baggins deserves."

"No!" said Thorin. "There is more in you of good than you know, child of the kindly West. Some courage and some wisdom, blended in measure. If more of us valued food and cheer and song above hoarded gold, it would be a merrier world. But sad or merry, I must leave it now. Farewell!"

Then Bilbo turned away, and he went by himself, and sat alone wrapped in a blanket, and, whether you believe it or not, he wept until his eyes were red and his voice was hoarse. He was a kindly little soul. Indeed it was long before he had the heart to make a joke again. "A mercy it is," he said at last to himself, "that I woke up when I did. I wish Thorin were living, but I am glad that we parted in kindness. You are a fool, Bilbo Baggins, and you made a great mess of that business with the stone; and there was a battle, in spite of all your efforts to buy peace and quiet, but I suppose you can hardly be blamed for that."

All that had happened after he was stunned, Bilbo learnt later; but it gave him more sorrow than joy, and he was now weary of his adventure. He was aching in his bones for the homeward journey. That, however, was a little delayed, so in the meantime I will tell something of events. The Eagles had long had suspicion of the goblins' mustering; from their watchfulness the movements in the mountains could not be altogether hid. So they too had gathered in great numbers, under the great Eagle of the Misty Mountains; and at length smelling battle from afar they had come speeding down the gale in the nick of time. They it was who dislodged the goblins from the mountain-slopes, casting them over precipices, or driving them down shrieking and bewildered among their foes. It was not long before they had freed the Lonely Mountain, and elves and men on either side of the valley could come at last to the help of the battle below.

But even with the Eagles they were still outnumbered. In that last hour Beorn himself had appeared – no one knew how or from where. He came alone, and in bear's shape; and he seemed to have grown almost to giant-size in his wrath.

The roar of his voice was like drums and guns; and he tossed wolves and goblins from his path like straws and feathers. He fell upon their rear, and broke like a clap of thunder through the ring. The dwarves were making a stand still about their lords upon a low rounded hill. Then Beorn stooped and lifted Thorin, who had fallen pierced with spears, and bore him out of the fray.

Swiftly he returned and his wrath was redoubled, so that nothing could withstand him, and no weapon seemed to bite upon him. He scattered the bodyguard, and pulled down Bolg himself and crushed him. Then dismay fell on the goblins and they fled in all directions. But weariness left their enemies with the coming of new hope, and they pursued them closely, and prevented most of them from escaping where they could. They drove many of them into the Running River, and such as fled south or west they hunted into the marshes about the Forest River; and there the greater part of the last fugitives perished, while those that came hardly to the Wood-elves' realm were there slain, or drawn in to die deep in the trackless dark of Mirkwood. Songs have said that three parts of the goblin warriors of the North perished on that day, and the mountains had peace for many a year.

Victory had been assured before the fall of night, but the pursuit was still on foot, when Bilbo returned to the camp; and not many were in the valley save the more grievously wounded.

"Where are the Eagles?" he asked Gandalf that evening, as he lay wrapped in many warm blankets.

"Some are in the hunt," said the wizard, "but most have gone back to their eyries. They would not stay here, and departed with the first light of morning. Dain has crowned their chief with gold, and sworn friendship with them for ever."

"I am sorry. I mean, I should have liked to see them again," said Bilbo sleepily; "perhaps I shall see them on the way home. I suppose I shall be going home soon?"

"As soon as you like," said the wizard.

Actually it was some days before Bilbo really set out. They buried Thorin deep beneath the Mountain, and Bard laid the Arkenstone upon his breast.

"There let it lie till the Mountain falls!" he said. "May it bring good fortune to all his folk that dwell here after!"

Upon his tomb the Elvenking then laid Orcrist, the elvish sword that had been taken from Thorin in captivity. It is said in songs that it gleamed ever in the dark if foes approached, and the fortress of the dwarves could not be taken by surprise. There now Dain son of Nain took up his abode, and he became King under the Mountain, and in time many other dwarves gathered to his throne in the ancient halls. Of the twelve companions of Thorin, ten remained. Fili and Kili had fallen defending him with shield and body, for he was their mother's eldest brother. The others remained with Dain; for Dain dealt his treasure well.

There was, of course, no longer any question of dividing the hoard in such shares as had been planned, to Balin and Dwalin, and Dori and Nori and Ori, and Oin and Gloin, and Bifur and Bofur and Bombur – or to Bilbo. Yet a fourteenth share of all the silver and gold, wrought and unwrought, was given up to Bard; for Dain said: "We will honour the agreement of the dead, and he has now the Arkenstone in his keeping."

Even a fourteenth share was wealth exceedingly great, greater than that of many mortal kings. From that treasure Bard sent much gold to the Master of Lake-town; and he rewarded his followers and friends freely. To the Elvenking he gave the emeralds of Girion, such jewels as he most loved, which Dain had restored to him.

To Bilbo he said: "This treasure is as much yours as it is mine; though old agreements cannot stand, since so many have a claim in its winning and defence. Yet even though you were willing to lay aside all your claim, I should wish that the words of Thorin, of which he repented, should not prove true: that we should give you little. I would reward you most richly of all."

"Very kind of you," said Bilbo. "But really it is a relief to me. How on earth should I have got all that treasure home without war and murder all along the way, I don't know. And I don't know what I should have done with it when I got home. I am sure it is better in your hands."

In the end he would only take two small chests, one filled with silver, and the other with gold, such as one strong pony could carry. "That will be quite as much as I can manage," said he.

At last the time came for him to say goodbye to his friends. "Farewell, Balin!" he said, "and farewell, Dwalin; and farewell Dori, Nori, Ori, Oin, Gloin, Bifur, Bofur, and Bombur! May your beards never grow thin!" And turning towards the Mountain he added: "Farewell Thorin Oakenshield! And Fili and Kili! May your memory never fade!"

Then the dwarves bowed low before their Gate, but words stuck in their throats. "Goodbye and good luck, wherever you fare!" said Balin at last. "If ever you visit us again, when our halls are made fair once more, then the feast shall indeed be splendid!"

"If ever you are passing my way," said Bilbo, "don't wait to knock! Tea is at four; but any of you are welcome at any time!"

Then he turned away.

The elf-host was on the march; and if it was sadly lessened, yet many were glad, for now the northern world would be merrier for many a long day. The dragon was dead, and the goblins overthrown, and their hearts looked forward after winter to a spring of joy.

Gandalf and Bilbo rode behind the Elvenking, and beside

them strode Beorn, once again in man's shape, and he laughed and sang in a loud voice upon the road. So they went on until they drew near to the borders of Mirkwood, to the north of the place where the Forest River ran out. Then they halted, for the wizard and Bilbo would not enter the wood, even though the king bade them stay a while in his halls. They intended to go along the edge of the forest, and round its northern end in the waste that lay between it and the beginning of the Grey Mountains. It was a long and cheerless road, but now that the goblins were crushed, it seemed safer to them than the dreadful pathways under the trees. Moreover Beorn was going that way too.

"Farewell! O Elvenking!" said Gandalf. "Merry be the greenwood, while the world is yet young! And merry be all your folk!"

"Farewell! O Gandalf!" said the king. "May you ever appear where you are most needed and least expected! The oftener you appear in my halls the better shall I be pleased!"

"I beg of you," said Bilbo stammering and standing on one foot, "to accept this gift!" and he brought out a necklace of silver and pearls that Dain had given him at their parting.

"In what way have I earned such a gift, O hobbit?" said the king.

"Well, er, I thought, don't you know," said Bilbo rather confused, "that, er, some little return should be made for your, er, hospitality. I mean even a burglar has his feelings. I have drunk much of your wine and eaten much of your bread."

"I will take your gift, O Bilbo the Magnificent!" said the

king gravely. "And I name you elf-friend and blessed. May your shadow never grow less (or stealing would be too easy)! Farewell!"

Then the elves turned towards the Forest, and Bilbo started on his long road home.

He had many hardships and adventures before he got back. The Wild was still the Wild, and there were many other things in it in those days beside goblins; but he was well guided and well guarded – the wizard was with him, and Beorn for much of the way – and he was never in great danger again. Anyway by midwinter Gandalf and Bilbo had come all the way back, along both edges of the Forest, to the doors of Beorn's house; and there for a while they both stayed. Yuletide was warm and merry there; and men came from far and wide to feast at Beorn's bidding. The goblins of the Misty Mountains were now few and terrified, and hidden in the deepest holes they could find; and the Wargs had vanished from the woods, so that men went abroad without fear. Beorn indeed became a great chief afterwards in those regions and ruled a wide land between the mountains and the wood; and it is said that for many generations the men of his line had the power of taking bear's shape, and some were grim men and bad, but most were in heart like Beorn, if less in size and strength. In their day the last goblins were hunted from the Misty Mountains and a new peace came over the edge of the Wild.

It was spring, and a fair one with mild weathers and a bright sun, before Bilbo and Gandalf took their leave at last of Beorn, and though he longed for home, Bilbo left with regret, for the flowers of the gardens of Beorn were in springtime no less marvellous than in high summer.

At last they came up the long road, and reached the very pass where the goblins had captured them before. But they came to that high point at morning, and looking backward they saw a white sun shining over the outstretched lands. There behind lay Mirkwood, blue in the distance, and darkly green at the nearer edge even in the spring. There far away was the Lonely Mountain on the edge of eyesight. On its highest peak snow yet unmelted was gleaming pale.

"So comes snow after fire, and even dragons have their ending!" said Bilbo, and he turned his back on his adventure. The Tookish part was getting very tired, and the Baggins was daily getting stronger. "I wish now only to be in my own armchair!" he said.

Chapter 19

THE LAST STAGE

IT WAS ON May the first that the two came back at last to the brink of the valley of Rivendell, where stood the Last (or the First) Homely House. Again it was evening, their ponies were tired, especially the one that carried the baggage; and they all felt in need of rest. As they rode down the steep path, Bilbo heard the elves still singing in the trees, as if they had not stopped since he left; and as soon as the riders came down into the lower glades of the wood they burst into song of much the same kind as before. This is something like it:

The dragon is withered,
His bones are now crumbled;
His armour is shivered,
His splendour is humbled!
Though sword shall be rusted,

And throne and crown perish
With strength that men trusted
And wealth that they cherish,
Here grass is still growing,
And leaves are yet swinging,
The white water flowing,
And elves are yet singing
Come! Tra-la-la-lally!
Come back to the valley!

The stars are far brighter
Than gems without measure,
The moon is far whiter
Than silver in treasure:
The fire is more shining
On hearth in the gloaming,
Than gold won by mining,
So why go a-roaming?
O! Tra-la-la-lally
Come back to the valley.

O! Where are you going,
So late in returning?
The river is flowing,
The stars are all burning!
O! Whither so laden
So sad and so dreary?
Here elf and elf-maiden

Now welcome the weary
With Tra-la-la-lally
Come back to the valley,
Tra-la-la-lally
Fa-la-la-lally
Fa-la!

Then the elves of the valley came out and greeted them and led them across the water to the house of Elrond. There a warm welcome was made them, and there were many eager ears that evening to hear the tale of their adventures. Gandalf it was who spoke, for Bilbo was fallen quiet and drowsy. Most of the tale he knew, for he had been in it, and had himself told much of it to the wizard on their homeward way or in the house of Beorn; but every now and again he would open one eye, and listen, when a part of the story which he did not yet know came in.

It was in this way that he learnt where Gandalf had been to; for he overheard the words of the wizard to Elrond. It appeared that Gandalf had been to a great council of the white wizards, masters of lore and good magic; and that they had at last driven the Necromancer from his dark hold in the south of Mirkwood.

"Ere long now," Gandalf was saying, "the Forest will grow somewhat more wholesome. The North will be freed from that horror for many long years, I hope. Yet I wish he were banished from the world!"

"It would be well indeed," said Elrond, "but I fear that will not come about in this age of the world, or for many after."

When the tale of their journeyings was told, there were other tales, and yet more tales, tales of long ago, and tales of new things, and tales of no time at all, till Bilbo's head fell forward on his chest, and he snored comfortably in a corner.

He woke to find himself in a white bed, and the moon shining through an open window. Below it many elves were singing loud and clear on the banks of the stream.

Sing all ye joyful, now sing all together!
The wind's in the tree-top, the wind's in the heather,
The stars are in blossom, the moon is in flower,
And bright are the windows of Night in her tower.

Dance all ye joyful, now dance all together!
Soft is the grass, and let foot be like feather!
The river is silver, the shadows are fleeting;
Merry is May-time, and merry our meeting.

Sing we now softly, and dreams let us weave him!
Wind him in slumber and there let us leave him!
The wanderer sleepeth. Now soft be his pillow!

Lullaby! Lullaby! Alder and Willow!
Sigh no more Pine, till the wind of the morn!
Fall Moon! Dark be the land!
Hush! Hush! Oak, Ash, and Thorn!
Hushed be all water, till dawn is at hand!

* * *

"Well, Merry People!" said Bilbo looking out. "What time by the moon is this? Your lullaby would waken a drunken goblin! Yet I thank you."

"And your snores would waken a stone dragon – yet we thank you," they answered with laughter. "It is drawing towards dawn, and you have slept now since the night's beginning. Tomorrow, perhaps, you will be cured of weariness."

"A little sleep does a great cure in the house of Elrond," said he; "but I will take all the cure I can get. A second good night, fair friends!" And with that he went back to bed and slept till late morning.

Weariness fell from him soon in that house, and he had many a merry jest and dance, early and late, with the elves of the valley. Yet even that place could not long delay him now, and he thought always of his own home. After a week, therefore, he said farewell to Elrond, and giving him such small gifts as he would accept, he rode away with Gandalf.

Even as they left the valley the sky darkened in the West before them, and wind and rain came up to meet them.

"Merry is May-time!" said Bilbo, as the rain beat into his face. "But our back is to legends and we are coming home. I suppose this is the first taste of it."

"There is a long road yet," said Gandalf.

"But it is the last road," said Bilbo.

They came to the river that marked the very edge of the borderland of the Wild, and to the ford beneath the steep bank, which you may remember. The water was swollen both with the melting of the snows at the approach of summer, and with the daylong rain; but they crossed with some difficulty, and pressed forward, as evening fell, on the last stage of their journey.

This was much as it had been before, except that the company was smaller, and more silent; also this time there were no trolls. At each point on the road Bilbo recalled the happenings and the words of a year ago – it seemed to him more like ten – so that, of course, he quickly noted the place where the pony had fallen in the river, and they had turned aside for their nasty adventure with Tom and Bert and Bill.

Not far from the road they found the gold of the trolls, which they had buried, still hidden and untouched. "I have enough to last me my time," said Bilbo, when they had dug it up. "You had better take this, Gandalf. I daresay you can find a use for it."

"Indeed I can!" said the wizard. "But share and share alike! You may find you have more needs than you expect."

So they put the gold in bags and slung them on the ponies, who were not at all pleased about it. After that their going was slower, for most of the time they walked. But the land was green and there was much grass through which the hobbit strolled along contentedly. He mopped his face with a red silk handkerchief – no! not a single one of his own had survived, he had borrowed this one from Elrond – for now June had brought summer, and the weather was bright and hot again.

As all things come to an end, even this story, a day came at last when they were in sight of the country where Bilbo had been born and bred, where the shapes of the land and of the trees were as well known to him as his hands and toes. Coming to a rise he could see his own Hill in the distance, and he stopped suddenly and said:

Roads go ever ever on,
Over rock and under tree,
By caves where never sun has shone,
By streams that never find the sea:
Over snow by winter sown,
And through the merry flowers of June,
Over grass and over stone,
And under mountains in the moon.

Roads go ever ever on
Under cloud and under star,
Yet feet that wandering have gone
Turn at last to home afar.
Eyes that fire and sword have seen
And horror in the halls of stone
Look at last on meadows green
And trees and hills they long have known.

Gandalf looked at him. "My dear Bilbo!" he said. "Something is the matter with you! You are not the hobbit that you were."

And so they crossed the bridge and passed the mill by the

river and came right back to Bilbo's own door.

"Bless me! What's going on?" he cried. There was a great commotion, and people of all sorts, respectable and unrespectable, were thick round the door, and many were going in and out – not even wiping their feet on the mat, as Bilbo noticed with annoyance.

If he was surprised, they were more surprised still. He had arrived back in the middle of an auction! There was a large notice in black and red hung on the gate, stating that on June the twenty-second Messrs Grubb, Grubb, and Burrowes would sell by auction the effects of the late Bilbo Baggins Esquire, of Bag-End, Underhill, Hobbiton. Sale to commence at ten o'clock sharp. It was now nearly lunch-time, and most of the things had already been sold, for various prices from next to nothing to old songs (as is not unusual at auctions). Bilbo's cousins the Sackville-Bagginses were, in fact, busy measuring his rooms to see if their own furniture would fit. In short Bilbo was "Presumed Dead", and not everybody that said so was sorry to find the presumption wrong.

The return of Mr Bilbo Baggins created quite a disturbance, both under the Hill and over the Hill, and across the Water; it was a great deal more than a nine days' wonder. The legal bother, indeed, lasted for years. It was quite a long time before Mr Baggins was in fact admitted to be alive again. The people who had got specially good bargains at the sale took a deal of convincing; and in the end to save time Bilbo had to buy back quite a lot of his own furniture. Many of his silver spoons mysteriously disappeared and were never accounted for. Personally he suspected the Sackville-Bagginses. On their side they never admitted that the returned Baggins was genuine, and they were not on friendly terms with Bilbo ever after. They really had wanted to live in his nice hobbit-hole so very much.

Indeed Bilbo found he had lost more than spoons – he had lost his reputation. It is true that for ever after he remained an elf-friend, and had the honour of dwarves, wizards, and all such folk as ever passed that way; but he was no longer quite respectable. He was in fact held by all the hobbits of the neighbourhood to be "queer" – except by his nephews and nieces on the Took side, but even they were not encouraged in their friendship by their elders.

I am sorry to say he did not mind. He was quite content; and the sound of the kettle on his hearth was ever after more musical than it had been even in the quiet days before the Unexpected Party. His sword he hung over the mantelpiece. His coat of mail was arranged on a stand in the hall (until he lent it to a museum). His gold and silver was largely spent in presents, both useful and extravagant – which to a certain extent accounts for the affection of his nephews and his nieces. His magic ring he kept a great secret, for he chiefly used it when unpleasant callers came.

He took to writing poetry and visiting the elves; and though many shook their heads and touched their foreheads and said "Poor old Baggins!" and though few believed any of his tales, he remained very happy to the end of his days, and those were extraordinarily long.

* * *

One autumn evening some years afterwards Bilbo was sitting in his study writing his memoirs – he thought of calling them "There and Back Again, a Hobbit's Holiday" – when there was a ring at the door. It was Gandalf and a dwarf; and the dwarf was actually Balin.

"Come in! come in!" said Bilbo, and soon they were settled in chairs by the fire. If Balin noticed that Mr Baggins' waistcoat was more extensive (and had real gold buttons), Bilbo also noticed that Balin's beard was several inches longer, and his jewelled belt was of great magnificence.

They fell to talking of their times together, of course, and Bilbo asked how things were going in the lands of the Mountain. It seemed they were going very well. Bard had rebuilt the town in Dale and men had gathered to him from the Lake and from South and West, and all the valley had become tilled again and rich, and the desolation was now filled with birds and blossoms in spring and fruit and feasting in the autumn. And Lake-town was refounded and was more prosperous than ever, and much wealth went up and down the Running River; and there was friendship in those parts between elves and dwarves and men.

The old Master had come to a bad end. Bard had given him much gold for the help of the Lake-people, but being of the kind that easily catches such disease he fell under the dragon-sickness, and took most of the gold and fled with it, and died of starvation in the Waste, deserted by his companions.

"The new Master is of wiser kind," said Balin, "and very popular, for, of course, he gets most of the credit for the present prosperity. They are making songs which say that in his day the rivers run with gold."

"Then the prophecies of the old songs have turned out to be true, after a fashion!" said Bilbo.

"Of course!" said Gandalf. "And why should not they prove true? Surely you don't disbelieve the prophecies, because you had a hand in bringing them about yourself? You don't really suppose, do you, that all your adventures and escapes were managed by mere luck, just for your sole benefit? You are a very fine person, Mr Baggins, and I am very fond of you; but you are only quite a little fellow in a wide world after all!"

"Thank goodness!" said Bilbo laughing, and handed him the tobacco-jar.

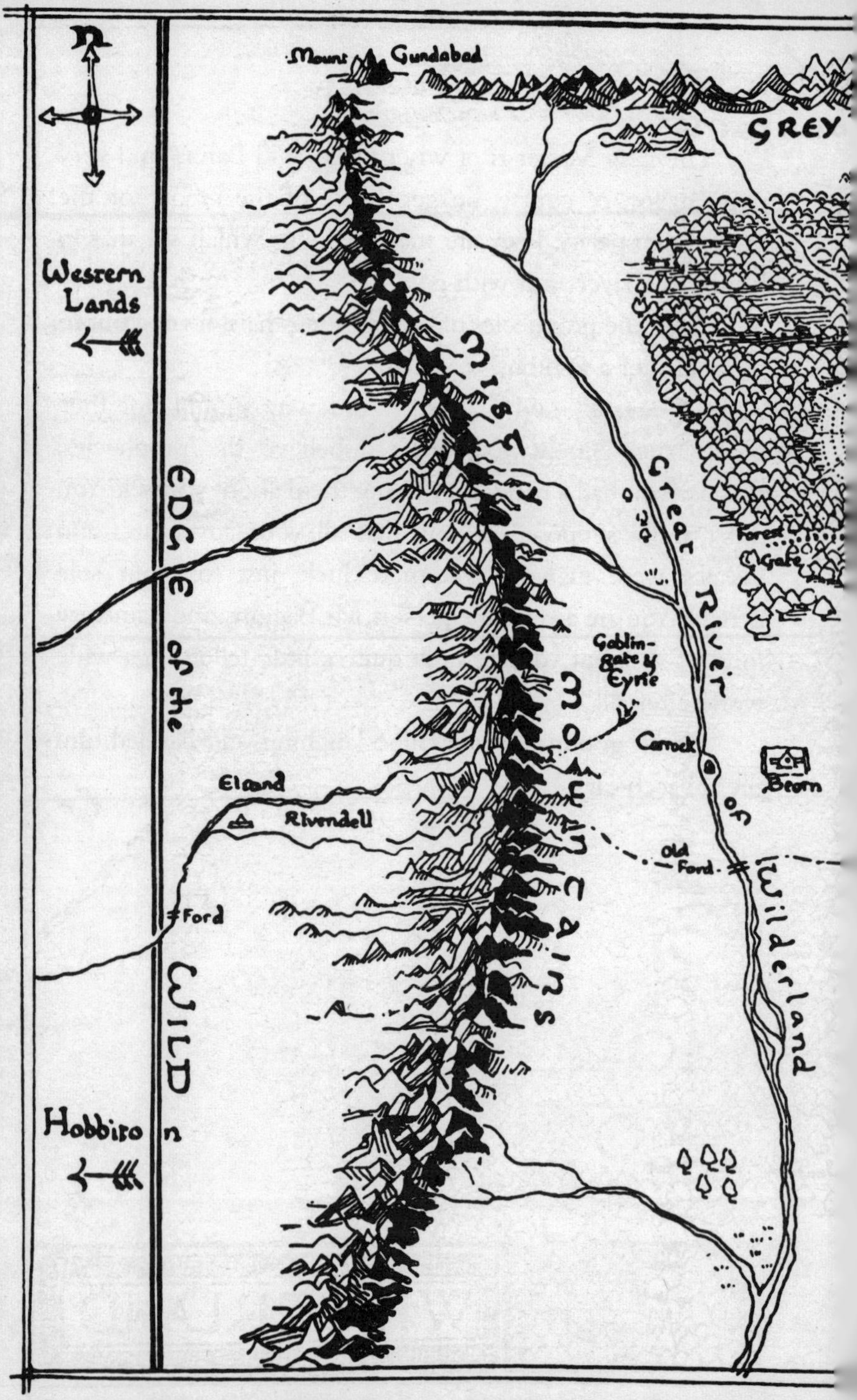
Mount Gundabad
GREY
Western Lands
Misty Mountains
EDGE of the WILD
Great River of Wilderland
Forest Gate
Goblin-gate & Eyrie
Carrock
Beorn
Old Ford
Elrond
Rivendell
Ford
Hobbiton

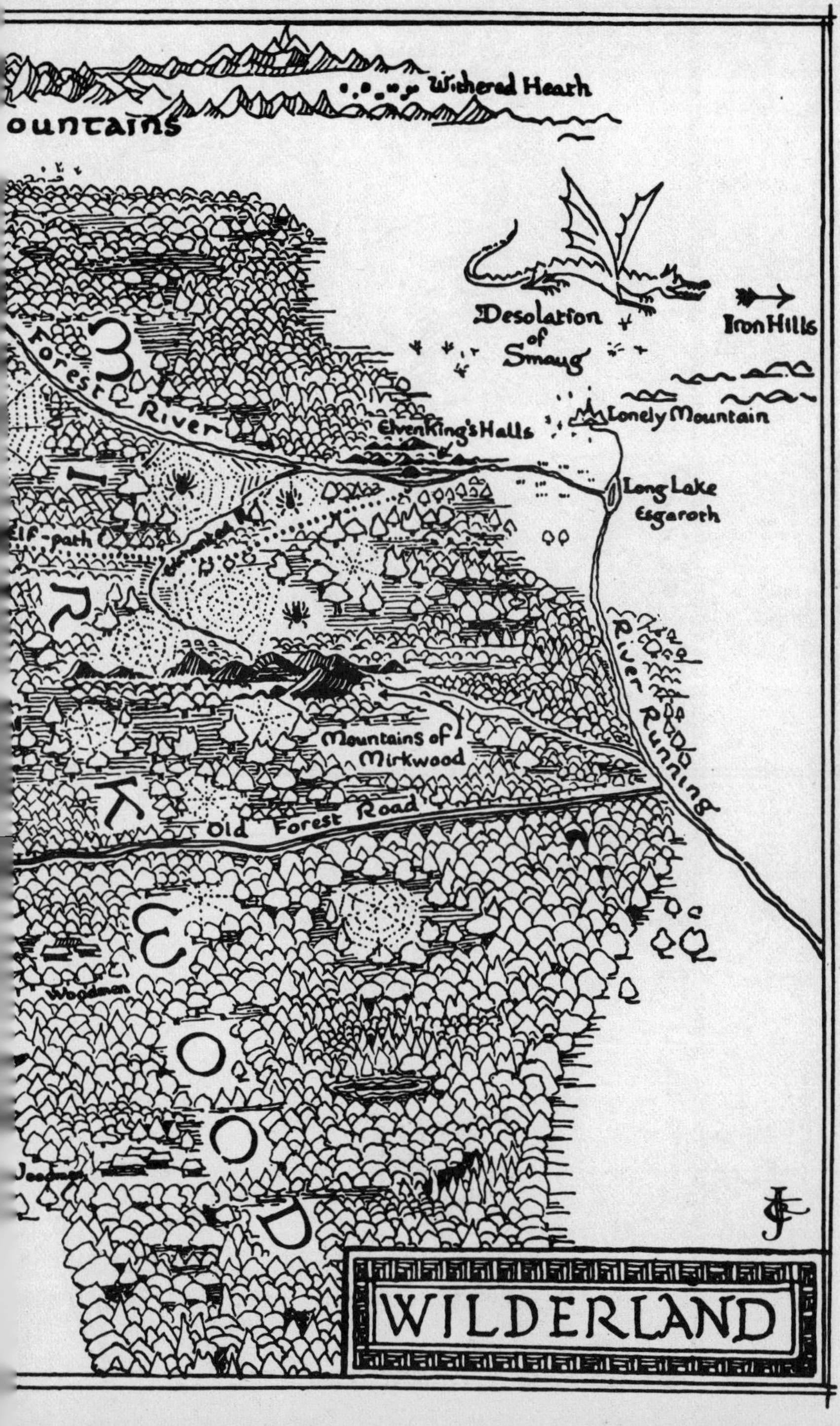

ountains
Withered Heath
Desolation of Smaug
Iron Hills
Lonely Mountain
Elvenking's Halls
Long Lake
Esgaroth
Forest River
Elf-path
River Running
Mountains of Mirkwood
Old Forest Road
Woodmen
WILDERLAND

Read on for the first chapter of

THE LORD OF THE RINGS

Three Rings for the Elven-kings under the sky,
Seven for the Dwarf-lords in their halls of stone,
Nine for Mortal Men doomed to die,
One for the Dark Lord on his dark throne
In the Land of Mordor where the Shadows lie.
One Ring to rule them all, One Ring to find them,
One Ring to bring them all and in the darkness bind them
In the Land of Mordor where the Shadows lie.

CHAPTER I

A LONG-EXPECTED PARTY

When Mr. Bilbo Baggins of Bag End announced that he would shortly be celebrating his eleventy-first birthday with a party of special magnificence, there was much talk and excitement in Hobbiton.

Bilbo was very rich and very peculiar, and had been the wonder of the Shire for sixty years, ever since his remarkable disappearance and unexpected return. The riches he had brought back from his travels had now become a local legend, and it was popularly believed, whatever the old folk might say, that the Hill at Bag End was full of tunnels stuffed with treasure. And if that was not enough for fame, there was also his prolonged vigour to marvel at. Time wore on, but it seemed to have little effect on Mr. Baggins. At ninety he was much the same as at fifty. At ninety-nine they began to call him *well-preserved*; but *unchanged* would have been nearer the mark. There were some that shook their heads and thought this was too much of a good thing; it seemed unfair that anyone should possess (apparently) perpetual youth as well as (reputedly) inexhaustible wealth.

'It will have to be paid for,' they said. 'It isn't natural, and trouble will come of it!'

But so far trouble had not come; and as Mr. Baggins was generous with his money, most people were willing to forgive him his oddities and his good fortune. He remained on visiting terms with his relatives (except, of course, the Sackville-Bagginses), and he had many devoted admirers among the hobbits of poor and unimportant families. But he had no close friends, until some of his younger cousins began to grow up.

The eldest of these, and Bilbo's favourite, was young Frodo Baggins. When Bilbo was ninety-nine he adopted Frodo as his heir, and brought him to live at Bag End; and the hopes of the Sackville-Bagginses were finally dashed. Bilbo and Frodo happened to have the same birthday, September 22nd. 'You had better come and live here, Frodo my lad,' said Bilbo one day; 'and then we can celebrate our birthday-parties comfortably together.' At that time Frodo was still in his *tweens*, as the hobbits called the irresponsible twenties between childhood and coming of age at thirty-three.

Twelve more years passed. Each year the Bagginses had given very lively combined birthday-parties at Bag End; but now it was understood that something quite exceptional was being planned for that autumn. Bilbo was going to be *eleventy-one*, 111, a rather curious number, and a very respectable age for a hobbit (the Old Took himself had only reached 130); and Frodo was going to be *thirty-three*, 33, an important number: the date of his 'coming of age'.

Tongues began to wag in Hobbiton and Bywater; and rumour of the coming event travelled all over the Shire. The history and character of Mr. Bilbo Baggins became once again the chief topic of conversation; and the older folk suddenly found their reminiscences in welcome demand.

No one had a more attentive audience than old Ham Gamgee, commonly known as the Gaffer. He held forth at *The Ivy Bush*, a small inn on the Bywater road; and he spoke with some authority, for he had tended the garden at Bag End for forty years, and had helped old Holman in the same job before that. Now that he was himself growing old and stiff in the joints, the job was mainly carried on by his youngest son, Sam Gamgee. Both father and son were on very friendly terms with Bilbo and Frodo. They lived on the Hill itself, in Number 3 Bagshot Row just below Bag End.

'A very nice well-spoken gentlehobbit is Mr. Bilbo, as I've always said,' the Gaffer declared. With perfect truth: for Bilbo was very polite to him, calling him 'Master Hamfast', and consulting him constantly upon the growing of vegetables – in the matter of 'roots', especially potatoes, the Gaffer was recognized as the leading authority by all in the neighbourhood (including himself).

'But what about this Frodo that lives with him?' asked Old Noakes of Bywater. 'Baggins is his name, but he's more than half a Brandybuck, they say. It beats me why any Baggins of Hobbiton should go looking for a wife away there in Buckland, where folks are so queer.'

'And no wonder they're queer,' put in Daddy Twofoot (the Gaffer's next-door neighbour), 'if they live on the wrong side of the Brandywine River, and right agin the Old Forest. That's a dark bad place, if half the tales be true.'

'You're right, Dad!' said the Gaffer. 'Not that the Brandybucks of Buckland live *in* the Old Forest; but they're a queer breed, seemingly. They fool about with boats on that big river – and that isn't natural. Small wonder that trouble came of it, I say. But be that as it may, Mr. Frodo is as nice a young hobbit as you could wish to meet. Very much like Mr. Bilbo, and in more than looks. After all his father was a Baggins. A decent respectable hobbit was Mr. Drogo Baggins; there was never much to tell of him, till he was drownded.'

'Drownded?' said several voices. They had heard this and other darker rumours before, of course; but hobbits have a passion for family history, and they were ready to hear it again.

'Well, so they say,' said the Gaffer. 'You see: Mr. Drogo, he married poor Miss Primula Brandybuck. She was our Mr. Bilbo's first cousin on the mother's side (her mother being the youngest of the Old Took's daughters); and Mr. Drogo was his second cousin. So Mr. Frodo is his first *and* second cousin, once removed either way, as the saying is, if you follow me. And Mr. Drogo was staying at Brandy Hall with his father-in-law, old Master Gorbadoc, as he often did after his marriage (him being partial to his vittles, and old Gorbadoc keeping a mighty generous table); and he went out *boat-*

ing on the Brandywine River; and he and his wife were drownded, and poor Mr. Frodo only a child and all.'

'I've heard they went on the water after dinner in the moonlight,' said Old Noakes; 'and it was Drogo's weight as sunk the boat.'

'And *I* heard she pushed him in, and he pulled her in after him,' said Sandyman, the Hobbiton miller.

'You shouldn't listen to all you hear, Sandyman,' said the Gaffer, who did not much like the miller. 'There isn't no call to go talking of pushing and pulling. Boats are quite tricky enough for those that sit still without looking further for the cause of trouble. Anyway: there was this Mr. Frodo left an orphan and stranded, as you might say, among those queer Bucklanders, being brought up anyhow in Brandy Hall. A regular warren, by all accounts. Old Master Gorbadoc never had fewer than a couple of hundred relations in the place. Mr. Bilbo never did a kinder deed than when he brought the lad back to live among decent folk.

'But I reckon it was a nasty shock for those Sackville-Bagginses. They thought they were going to get Bag End, that time when he went off and was thought to be dead. And then he comes back and orders them off; and he goes on living and living, and never looking a day older, bless him! And suddenly he produces an heir, and has all the papers made out proper. The Sackville-Bagginses won't never see the inside of Bag End now, or it is to be hoped not.'

'There's a tidy bit of money tucked away up there, I hear tell,' said a stranger, a visitor on business from Michel Delving in the Westfarthing. 'All the top of your hill is full of tunnels packed with chests of gold and silver, *and* jools, by what I've heard.'

'Then you've heard more than I can speak to,' answered the Gaffer. 'I know nothing about *jools*. Mr. Bilbo is free with his money, and there seems no lack of it; but I know of no tunnel-making. I saw Mr. Bilbo when he came back, a matter of sixty years ago, when I was a lad. I'd not long come prentice to old Holman (him being my dad's cousin), but he had me up at Bag End helping him to keep folks from trampling and trapessing all over the garden while the sale was on. And in the middle of it all Mr. Bilbo comes up the Hill with a pony and some mighty big bags and a couple of chests. I don't doubt they were mostly full of treasure he had picked up in foreign parts, where there be mountains of gold, they say; but there wasn't enough to fill tunnels. But my lad Sam will know more about that. He's in and out of Bag End. Crazy about stories of the old days he is, and he listens to all Mr. Bilbo's tales. Mr. Bilbo has learned him his letters – meaning no harm, mark you, and I hope no harm will come of it.

'*Elves and Dragons!* I says to him. *Cabbages and potatoes are better for me and you. Don't go getting mixed up in the business of your betters, or you'll land in trouble too big for you,* I says to him. And I might say it to others,' he added with a look at the stranger and the miller.

But the Gaffer did not convince his audience. The legend of Bilbo's wealth was now too firmly fixed in the minds of the younger generation of hobbits.

'Ah, but he has likely enough been adding to what he brought at first,' argued the miller, voicing common opinion. 'He's often away from home. And look at the outlandish folk that visit him: dwarves coming at night, and that old wandering conjuror, Gandalf, and all. You can say what you like, Gaffer, but Bag End's a queer place, and its folk are queerer.'

'And you can say what *you* like, about what you know no more of than you do of boating, Mr. Sandyman,' retorted the Gaffer, disliking the miller even more than usual. 'If that's being queer, then we could do with a bit more queerness in these parts. There's some not far away that wouldn't offer a pint of beer to a friend, if they lived in a hole with golden walls. But they do things proper at Bag End. Our Sam says that *everyone's* going to be invited to the party, and there's going to be presents, mark you, presents for all – this very month as is.'

* * *

That very month was September, and as fine as you could ask. A day or two later a rumour (probably started by the knowledgeable Sam) was spread about that there were going to be fireworks – fireworks, what is more, such as had not been seen in the Shire for nigh on a century, not indeed since the Old Took died.

Days passed and The Day drew nearer. An odd-looking waggon laden with odd-looking packages rolled into Hobbiton one evening and toiled up the Hill to Bag End. The startled hobbits peered out of lamplit doors to gape at it. It was driven by outlandish folk, singing strange songs: dwarves with long beards and deep hoods. A few of them remained at Bag End. At the end of the second week in September a cart came in through Bywater from the direction of the Brandywine Bridge in broad daylight. An old man was driving it all alone. He wore a tall pointed blue hat, a long grey cloak, and a silver scarf. He had a long white beard and bushy eyebrows that stuck out beyond the brim of his hat. Small hobbit-children ran after the cart all through Hobbiton and right up the hill. It had a cargo of fireworks, as they rightly guessed. At Bilbo's front door the old man began to unload: there were great bundles of fireworks of all sorts and shapes, each labelled with a large red G  and the elf-rune, .

That was Gandalf's mark, of course, and the old man was Gandalf the Wizard, whose fame in the Shire was due mainly to his skill with fires, smokes, and lights. His real business was far more difficult and dangerous, but the Shire-folk knew nothing about it. To them he was just one of the 'attractions' at the Party. Hence the excitement of the hobbit-children. 'G for Grand!' they shouted, and the old man smiled. They knew him by sight, though he only appeared in Hobbiton occasionally and never stopped long; but neither they nor any but the oldest of their elders had seen one of his firework displays – they now belonged to the legendary past.

When the old man, helped by Bilbo and some dwarves, had finished unloading, Bilbo gave a few pennies away; but not a single squib or cracker was forthcoming, to the disappointment of the onlookers.

'Run away now!' said Gandalf. 'You will get plenty when the time comes.' Then he disappeared inside with Bilbo, and the door was shut. The young hobbits stared at the door in vain for a while, and then made off, feeling that the day of the party would never come.

Inside Bag End, Bilbo and Gandalf were sitting at the open window of a small room looking out west on to the garden. The late afternoon was bright and peaceful. The flowers glowed red and golden: snap-dragons and sunflowers, and nasturtians trailing all over the turf walls and peeping in at the round windows.

'How bright your garden looks!' said Gandalf.

'Yes,' said Bilbo. 'I am very fond indeed of it, and of all the dear old Shire; but I think I need a holiday.'

'You mean to go on with your plan then?'

'I do. I made up my mind months ago, and I haven't changed it.'

'Very well. It is no good saying any more. Stick to your plan – your whole plan, mind – and I hope it will turn out for the best, for you, and for all of us.'

'I hope so. Anyway I mean to enjoy myself on Thursday, and have my little joke.'

'Who will laugh, I wonder?' said Gandalf, shaking his head.

'We shall see,' said Bilbo.

The next day more carts rolled up the Hill, and still more carts. There might have been some grumbling about 'dealing locally', but that very week orders began to pour out of Bag End for every kind of provision, commodity, or luxury that could be obtained in Hobbiton or Bywater or anywhere in the neighbourhood. People became enthusiastic; and they began to tick off the days on the calendar; and they watched eagerly for the postman, hoping for invitations.

Before long the invitations began pouring out, and the

Hobbiton post-office was blocked, and the Bywater post-office was snowed under, and voluntary assistant postmen were called for. There was a constant stream of them going up the Hill, carrying hundreds of polite variations on *Thank you, I shall certainly come.*

A notice appeared on the gate at Bag End: NO ADMITTANCE EXCEPT ON PARTY BUSINESS. Even those who had, or pretended to have Party Business were seldom allowed inside. Bilbo was busy: writing invitations, ticking off answers, packing up presents, and making some private preparations of his own. From the time of Gandalf's arrival he remained hidden from view.

One morning the hobbits woke to find the large field, south of Bilbo's front door, covered with ropes and poles for tents and pavilions. A special entrance was cut into the bank leading to the road, and wide steps and a large white gate were built there. The three hobbit-families of Bagshot Row, adjoining the field, were intensely interested and generally envied. Old Gaffer Gamgee stopped even pretending to work in his garden.

The tents began to go up. There was a specially large pavilion, so big that the tree that grew in the field was right inside it, and stood proudly near one end, at the head of the chief table. Lanterns were hung on all its branches. More promising still (to the hobbits' mind): an enormous open-air kitchen was erected in the north corner of the field. A draught of cooks, from every inn and eating-house for miles around, arrived to supplement the dwarves and other odd folk that were quartered at Bag End. Excitement rose to its height.

Then the weather clouded over. That was on Wednesday the eve of the Party. Anxiety was intense. Then Thursday, September the 22nd, actually dawned. The sun got up, the clouds vanished, flags were unfurled and the fun began.

Bilbo Baggins called it a *party*, but it was really a variety of entertainments rolled into one. Practically everybody living near was invited. A very few were overlooked by accident, but as they turned up all the same, that did not matter. Many people from other parts of the Shire were also asked; and there were even a few from outside the borders. Bilbo met the guests (and additions) at the new white gate in person. He gave away presents to all and sundry – the latter were those who went out again by a back way and came in again by the gate. Hobbits give presents to other people on their own birthdays. Not very expensive ones, as a rule, and not so lavishly as on this occasion; but it was not a bad system. Actually in Hobbiton and Bywater every day in the year it was somebody's birthday, so that every hobbit in those parts had a fair chance of at least one present at least once a week. But they never got tired of them.

On this occasion the presents were unusually good. The hobbit-children were so excited that for a while they almost forgot about eating. There were toys the like of which they had never seen before, all beautiful and some obviously magical. Many of them had indeed been ordered a year before, and had come all the way from the Mountain and from Dale, and were of real dwarf-make.

When every guest had been welcomed and was finally inside the gate, there were songs, dances, music, games, and, of course, food and drink. There were three official meals: lunch, tea, and dinner (or supper). But lunch and tea were marked chiefly by the fact that at those times all the guests were sitting down and eating together. At other times there were merely lots of people eating and drinking – continuously from elevenses until six-thirty, when the fireworks started.

The fireworks were by Gandalf: they were not only brought by him, but designed and made by him; and the special effects, set pieces, and flights of rockets were let off by him. But there was also a generous distribution of squibs, crackers, backarappers, sparklers, torches, dwarf-candles, elf-fountains, goblin-barkers and thunder-claps. They were all superb. The art of Gandalf improved with age.

There were rockets like a flight of scintillating birds singing with sweet voices. There were green trees with trunks of dark smoke: their leaves opened like a whole spring unfolding in a moment, and their shining branches dropped glowing flowers down upon the astonished hobbits, disappearing with a sweet scent just before they touched their upturned faces. There were fountains of butterflies that flew glittering into the trees; there were pillars of coloured fires that rose and turned into eagles, or sailing ships, or a phalanx of flying swans; there was a red thunderstorm and a shower of yellow rain; there was a forest of silver spears that sprang suddenly into the air with a yell like an embattled army, and came down again into the Water with a hiss like a hundred hot snakes. And there was also one last surprise, in honour of Bilbo, and it startled the hobbits exceedingly, as Gandalf intended. The lights went out. A great smoke went up. It shaped itself like a mountain seen in the distance, and began to glow at the summit. It spouted green and scarlet flames. Out flew a red-golden dragon – not life-size, but terribly life-like: fire came from his jaws, his eyes glared down; there was a roar, and he whizzed three times over the heads of the crowd. They all ducked, and many fell flat on their faces. The dragon passed like an express train, turned a somersault, and burst over Bywater with a deafening explosion.

'That is the signal for supper!' said Bilbo. The pain and alarm vanished at once, and the prostrate hobbits leaped to their feet. There was a splendid supper for everyone; for everyone, that is, except those invited to the special family dinner-party. This was held in the great pavilion with the tree. The invitations were limited to twelve dozen (a number also called by the hobbits one Gross, though the word was not considered proper to use of people); and the guests were selected from all the families to which Bilbo and Frodo were related, with the addition of a few special unrelated friends (such as Gandalf). Many young hobbits were included, and present by parental permission; for hobbits were easy-going with their children in the matter of sitting up late, especially when there was a chance of getting them a free meal. Bringing up young hobbits took a lot of provender.

There were many Bagginses and Boffins, and also many

Tooks and Brandybucks; there were various Grubbs (relations of Bilbo Baggins' grandmother), and various Chubbs (connexions of his Took grandfather); and a selection of Burrowses, Bolgers, Bracegirdles, Brockhouses, Goodbodies, Hornblowers and Proudfoots. Some of these were only very distantly connected with Bilbo, and some of them had hardly ever been in Hobbiton before, as they lived in remote corners of the Shire. The Sackville-Bagginses were not forgotten. Otho and his wife Lobelia were present. They disliked Bilbo and detested Frodo, but so magnificent was the invitation card, written in golden ink, that they had felt it was impossible to refuse. Besides, their cousin, Bilbo, had been specializing in food for many years and his table had a high reputation.

All the one hundred and forty-four guests expected a pleasant feast; though they rather dreaded the after-dinner speech of their host (an inevitable item). He was liable to drag in bits of what he called poetry; and sometimes, after a glass or two, would allude to the absurd adventures of his mysterious journey. The guests were not disappointed: they had a *very* pleasant feast, in fact an engrossing entertainment: rich, abundant, varied, and prolonged. The purchase of provisions fell almost to nothing throughout the district in the ensuing weeks; but as Bilbo's catering had depleted the stocks of most stores, cellars and warehouses for miles around, that did not matter much.

After the feast (more or less) came the Speech. Most of the company were, however, now in a tolerant mood, at that delightful stage which they called 'filling up the corners'. They were sipping their favourite drinks, and nibbling at their favourite dainties, and their fears were forgotten. They were prepared to listen to anything, and to cheer at every full stop.

My dear People, began Bilbo, rising in his place. 'Hear! Hear! Hear!' they shouted, and kept on repeating it in chorus, seeming reluctant to follow their own advice. Bilbo left his place and went and stood on a chair under the illuminated tree. The light of the lanterns fell on his beaming face; the golden buttons shone on his embroidered silk waistcoat. They could all see him standing, waving one hand in the air, the other was in his trouser-pocket.

My dear Bagginses and Boffins, he began again; *and my dear Tooks and Brandybucks, and Grubbs, and Chubbs, and Burrowses, and Hornblowers, and Bolgers, Bracegirdles, Goodbodies, Brockhouses and Proudfoots.* 'ProudFEET!' shouted an elderly hobbit from the back of the pavilion. His name, of course, was Proudfoot, and well merited; his feet were large, exceptionally furry, and both were on the table.

Proudfoots, repeated Bilbo. *Also my good Sackville-Bagginses that I welcome back at last to Bag End. Today is my one hundred and eleventh birthday: I am eleventy-one today!* 'Hurray! Hurray! Many Happy Returns!' they shouted, and they hammered joyously on the tables. Bilbo was doing splendidly. This was the sort of stuff they liked: short and obvious.

I hope you are all enjoying yourselves as much as I am. Deafening cheers. Cries of *Yes* (and *No*). Noises of trumpets and horns, pipes and flutes, and other musical instruments. There were, as has been said, many young hobbits present. Hundreds of musical crackers had been pulled. Most of them bore the mark DALE on them; which did not convey much to most of the hobbits, but they all agreed they were marvellous crackers. They contained instruments, small, but of perfect make and enchanting tones. Indeed, in one corner some of the young Tooks and Brandybucks, supposing Uncle Bilbo to have finished (since he had plainly said all that was necessary), now got up an impromptu orchestra, and began a merry dance-tune. Master Everard Took and Miss Melilot Brandybuck got on a table and with bells in their hands began to dance the Springle-ring: a pretty dance, but rather vigorous.

But Bilbo had not finished. Seizing a horn from a youngster near by, he blew three loud hoots. The noise subsided. *I shall not keep you long,* he cried. Cheers from all the assembly. *I have called you all together for a Purpose.* Something in the way that he said this made an impression. There was almost silence, and one or two of the Tooks pricked up their ears.

Indeed, for Three Purposes! First of all, to tell you that I am immensely fond of you all, and that eleventy-one years is too short a time to live among such excellent and admirable hobbits. Tremendous outburst of approval.

I don't know half of you half as well as I should like; and I like less than half of you half as well as you deserve. This was unexpected and rather difficult. There was some scattered clapping, but most of them were trying to work it out and see if it came to a compliment.

Secondly, to celebrate my birthday. Cheers again. *I should say: OUR birthday. For it is, of course, also the birthday of my heir and nephew, Frodo. He comes of age and into his inheritance today.* Some perfunctory clapping by the elders; and some loud shouts of 'Frodo! Frodo! Jolly old Frodo,' from the juniors. The Sackville-Bagginses scowled, and wondered what was meant by 'coming into his inheritance'.

Together we score one hundred and forty-four. Your numbers were chosen to fit this remarkable total: One Gross, if I may use the expression. No cheers. This was ridiculous. Many of his guests, and especially the Sackville-Bagginses, were insulted, feeling sure they had only been asked to fill up the required number, like goods in a package. 'One Gross, indeed! Vulgar expression.'

It is also, if I may be allowed to refer to ancient history, the anniversary of my arrival by barrel at Esgaroth on the Long Lake; though the fact that it was my birthday slipped my memory on that occasion. I was only fifty-one then, and birthdays did not seem so important. The banquet was very splendid, however, though I had a bad cold at the time, I remember, and could only say 'thag you very buch'. I now repeat it more correctly: Thank you very much for coming to my little party. Obstinate silence. They all feared that a song or some poetry was now imminent; and they were getting bored. Why couldn't he stop talking and let them drink his health? But Bilbo did not sing or recite. He paused for a moment.

Thirdly and finally, he said, *I wish to make an ANNOUNCEMENT.* He spoke this last word so loudly and suddenly that everyone sat up who still could. *I regret to announce that – though, as I said, eleventy-one years is far too short a time to spend among you – this is the END. I am going. I am leaving NOW. GOOD-BYE!*

He stepped down and vanished. There was a blinding flash of light, and the guests all blinked. When they opened their eyes Bilbo was nowhere to be seen. One hundred and forty-four flabbergasted hobbits sat back speechless. Old Odo Proudfoot removed his feet from the table and stamped. Then there was a dead silence, until suddenly, after several deep breaths, every Baggins, Boffin, Took, Brandybuck, Grubb, Chubb, Burrows, Bolger, Bracegirdle, Brockhouse, Goodbody, Hornblower, and Proudfoot began to talk at once.

It was generally agreed that the joke was in very bad taste, and more food and drink were needed to cure the guests of shock and annoyance. 'He's mad. I always said so,' was probably the most popular comment. Even the Tooks (with a few exceptions) thought Bilbo's behaviour was absurd. For the moment most of them took it for granted that his disappearance was nothing more than a ridiculous prank.

But old Rory Brandybuck was not so sure. Neither age nor an enormous dinner had clouded his wits, and he said to his daughter-in-law, Esmeralda: 'There's something fishy in this, my dear! I believe that mad Baggins is off again. Silly old fool. But why worry? He hasn't taken the vittles with him.' He called loudly to Frodo to send the wine round again.

Frodo was the only one present who had said nothing. For some time he had sat silent beside Bilbo's empty chair, and ignored all remarks and questions. He had enjoyed the joke, of course, even though he had been in the know. He had difficulty in keeping from laughter at the indignant surprise of the guests. But at the same time he felt deeply troubled: he realized suddenly that he loved the old hobbit dearly. Most of the guests went on eating and drinking and discussing

Bilbo Baggins' oddities, past and present; but the Sackville-Bagginses had already departed in wrath. Frodo did not want to have any more to do with the party. He gave orders for more wine to be served; then he got up and drained his own glass silently to the health of Bilbo, and slipped out of the pavilion.

As for Bilbo Baggins, even while he was making his speech, he had been fingering the golden ring in his pocket: his magic ring that he had kept secret for so many years. As he stepped down he slipped it on his finger, and he was never seen by any hobbit in Hobbiton again.

He walked briskly back to his hole, and stood for a moment listening with a smile to the din in the pavilion and to the sounds of merrymaking in other parts of the field. Then he went in. He took off his party clothes, folded up and wrapped in tissue-paper his embroidered silk waistcoat, and put it away. Then he put on quickly some old untidy garments, and fastened round his waist a worn leather belt. On it he hung a short sword in a battered black-leather scabbard. From a locked drawer, smelling of moth-balls, he took out an old cloak and hood. They had been locked up as if they were very precious, but they were so patched and weatherstained that their original colour could hardly be guessed: it might have been dark green. They were rather too large for him. He then went into his study, and from a large strong-box took out a bundle wrapped in old cloths, and a leather-bound manuscript; and also a large bulky envelope. The book and bundle he stuffed into the top of a heavy bag that was standing there, already nearly full. Into the envelope he slipped his golden ring, and its fine chain, and then sealed it, and addressed it to Frodo. At first he put it on the mantelpiece, but suddenly he removed it and stuck it in his pocket. At that moment the door opened and Gandalf came quickly in.

'Hullo!' said Bilbo. 'I wondered if you would turn up.'

'I am glad to find you visible,' replied the wizard, sitting down in a chair, 'I wanted to catch you and have a few final words. I suppose you feel that everything has gone off splendidly and according to plan?'

'Yes, I do,' said Bilbo. 'Though that flash was surprising: it quite startled me, let alone the others. A little addition of your own, I suppose?'

'It was. You have wisely kept that ring secret all these years, and it seemed to me necessary to give your guests something else that would seem to explain your sudden vanishment.'

'And would spoil my joke. You are an interfering old busybody,' laughed Bilbo, 'but I expect you know best, as usual.'

'I do – when I know anything. But I don't feel too sure about this whole affair. It has now come to the final point. You have had your joke, and alarmed or offended most of your relations, and given the whole Shire something to talk about for nine days, or ninety-nine more likely. Are you going any further?'

'Yes, I am. I feel I need a holiday, a very long holiday, as I have told you before. Probably a permanent holiday: I don't expect I shall return. In fact, I don't mean to, and I have made all arrangements.

'I am old, Gandalf. I don't look it, but I am beginning to feel it in my heart of hearts. *Well-preserved* indeed!' he snorted. 'Why, I feel all thin, sort of *stretched*, if you know what I mean: like butter that has been scraped over too much bread. That can't be right. I need a change, or something.'

Gandalf looked curiously and closely at him. 'No, it does not seem right,' he said thoughtfully. 'No, after all I believe your plan is probably the best.'

'Well, I've made up my mind, anyway. I want to see mountains again, Gandalf – *mountains*; and then find somewhere where I can *rest*. In peace and quiet, without a lot of relatives prying around, and a string of confounded visitors hanging on the bell. I might find somewhere where I can finish my book. I have thought of a nice ending for it: *and he lived happily ever after to the end of his days*.'

Gandalf laughed. 'I hope he will. But nobody will read the book, however it ends.'

'Oh, they may, in years to come. Frodo has read some already, as far as it has gone. You'll keep an eye on Frodo, won't you?'

'Yes, I will – two eyes, as often as I can spare them.'

'He would come with me, of course, if I asked him. In fact he offered to once, just before the party. But he does not really want to, yet. I want to see the wild country again before I die, and the Mountains; but he is still in love with the Shire, with woods and fields and little rivers. He ought to be comfortable here. I am leaving everything to him, of course, except a few oddments. I hope he will be happy, when he gets used to being on his own. It's time he was his own master now.'

'Everything?' said Gandalf. 'The ring as well? You agreed to that, you remember.'

'Well, er, yes, I suppose so,' stammered Bilbo.

'Where is it?'

'In an envelope, if you must know,' said Bilbo impatiently. 'There on the mantelpiece. Well, no! Here it is in my pocket!' He hesitated. 'Isn't that odd now?' he said softly to himself. 'Yet after all, why not? Why shouldn't it stay there?'

Gandalf looked again very hard at Bilbo, and there was a gleam in his eyes. 'I think, Bilbo,' he said quietly, 'I should leave it behind. Don't you want to?'

'Well yes – and no. Now it comes to it, I don't like parting with it at all, I may say. And I don't really see why I should. Why do you want me to?' he asked, and a curious change came over his voice. It was sharp with suspicion and annoyance. 'You are always badgering me about my ring; but you have never bothered me about the other things that I got on my journey.'

'No, but I had to badger you,' said Gandalf. 'I wanted the truth. It was important. Magic rings are – well, magical; and they are rare and curious. I was professionally interested in your ring, you may say; and I still am. I should like to know where it is, if you go wandering again. Also I think *you* have had it quite long enough. You won't need it any more, Bilbo, unless I am quite mistaken.'

Bilbo flushed, and there was an angry light in his eyes. His kindly face grew hard. 'Why not?' he cried. 'And what business is it of yours, anyway, to know what I do with my own things? It is my own. I found it. It came to me.'

'Yes, yes,' said Gandalf. 'But there is no need to get angry.'

'If I am it is your fault,' said Bilbo. 'It is mine, I tell you. My own. My precious. Yes, my precious.'

The wizard's face remained grave and attentive, and only a flicker in his deep eyes showed that he was startled and indeed alarmed. 'It has been called that before,' he said, 'but not by you.'

'But I say it now. And why not? Even if Gollum said the same once. It's not his now, but mine. And I shall keep it, I say.'

Gandalf stood up. He spoke sternly. 'You will be a fool if you do, Bilbo,' he said. 'You make that clearer with every word you say. It has got far too much hold on you. Let it go! And then you can go yourself, and be free.'

'I'll do as I choose and go as I please,' said Bilbo obstinately.

'Now, now, my dear hobbit!' said Gandalf. 'All your long life we have been friends, and you owe me something. Come! Do as you promised: give it up!'

'Well, if you want my ring yourself, say so!' cried Bilbo. 'But you won't get it. I won't give my precious away, I tell you.' His hand strayed to the hilt of his small sword.

Gandalf's eyes flashed. 'It will be my turn to get angry soon,' he said. 'If you say that again, I shall. Then you will see Gandalf the Grey uncloaked.' He took a step towards the hobbit, and he seemed to grow tall and menacing; his shadow filled the little room.

Bilbo backed away to the wall, breathing hard, his hand clutching at his pocket. They stood for a while facing one another, and the air of the room tingled. Gandalf's eyes remained bent on the hobbit. Slowly his hands relaxed, and he began to tremble.

'I don't know what has come over you, Gandalf,' he said. 'You have never been like this before. What is it all about? It is mine isn't it? I found it, and Gollum would have killed me, if I hadn't kept it. I'm not a thief, whatever he said.'

'I have never called you one,' Gandalf answered. 'And I am not one either. I am not trying to rob you, but to help you. I wish you would trust me, as you used.' He turned away, and the shadow passed. He seemed to dwindle again to an old grey man, bent and troubled.

Bilbo drew his hand over his eyes. 'I am sorry,' he said. 'But I felt so queer. And yet it would be a relief in a way not to be bothered with it any more. It has been so growing on my mind lately. Sometimes I have felt it was like an eye looking at me. And I am always wanting to put it on and disappear, don't you know; or wondering if it is safe, and pulling it out to make sure. I tried locking it up, but I found I couldn't rest without it in my pocket. I don't know why. And I don't seem able to make up my mind.'

'Then trust mine,' said Gandalf. 'It is quite made up. Go away and leave it behind. Stop possessing it. Give it to Frodo, and I will look after him.'

Bilbo stood for a moment tense and undecided. Presently he sighed. 'All right,' he said with an effort. 'I will.' Then he shrugged his shoulders, and smiled rather ruefully. 'After all that's what this party business was all about, really: to give away lots of birthday presents, and somehow make it easier to give it away at the same time. It hasn't made it any easier in the end, but it would be a pity to waste all my preparations. It would quite spoil the joke.'

'Indeed it would take away the only point I ever saw in the affair,' said Gandalf.

'Very well,' said Bilbo, 'it goes to Frodo with all the rest.' He drew a deep breath. 'And now I really must be starting, or somebody else will catch me. I have said good-bye, and I couldn't bear to do it all over again.' He picked up his bag and moved to the door.

'You have still got the ring in your pocket,' said the wizard.

'Well, so I have!' cried Bilbo. 'And my will and all the other documents too. You had better take it and deliver it for me. That will be safest.'

'No, don't give the ring to me,' said Gandalf. 'Put it on the mantelpiece. It will be safe enough there, till Frodo comes. I shall wait for him.'

Bilbo took out the envelope, but just as he was about to set it by the clock, his hand jerked back, and the packet fell on the floor. Before he could pick it up, the wizard stooped and seized it and set it in its place. A spasm of anger passed swiftly over the hobbit's face again. Suddenly it gave way to a look of relief and a laugh.

'Well, that's that,' he said. 'Now I'm off!'

They went out into the hall. Bilbo chose his favourite stick from the stand; then he whistled. Three dwarves came out of different rooms where they had been busy.

'Is everything ready?' asked Bilbo. 'Everything packed and labelled?'

'Everything,' they answered.

'Well, let's start then!' He stepped out of the front-door.

It was a fine night, and the black sky was dotted with stars. He looked up, sniffing the air. 'What fun! What fun to be off again, off on the Road with dwarves! This is what I have really been longing for, for years! Good-bye!' he said, looking at his old home and bowing to the door. 'Good-bye, Gandalf!'

'Good-bye, for the present, Bilbo. Take care of yourself! You are old enough, and perhaps wise enough.'

'Take care! I don't care. Don't you worry about me! I am as happy now as I have ever been, and that is saying a great deal. But the time has come. I am being swept off my feet at last,' he added, and then in a low voice, as if to himself, he sang softly in the dark:

The Road goes ever on and on
Down from the door where it began.
Now far ahead the Road has gone,
And I must follow, if I can,
Pursuing it with eager feet,
Until it joins some larger way
Where many paths and errands meet.
And whither then? I cannot say.

He paused, silent for a moment. Then without another word he turned away from the lights and voices in the fields and tents, and followed by his three companions went round into his garden, and trotted down the long sloping path. He jumped over a low place in the hedge at the bottom, and took to the meadows, passing into the night like a rustle of wind in the grass.

Gandalf remained for a while staring after him into the darkness. 'Good-bye, my dear Bilbo – until our next meeting!' he said softly and went back indoors.

Frodo came in soon afterwards, and found him sitting in the dark, deep in thought. 'Has he gone?' he asked.

'Yes,' answered Gandalf, 'he has gone at last.'

'I wish – I mean, I hoped until this evening that it was only a joke,' said Frodo. 'But I knew in my heart that he really meant to go. He always used to joke about serious things. I wish I had come back sooner, just to see him off.'

'I think really he preferred slipping off quietly in the end,' said Gandalf. 'Don't be too troubled. He'll be all right – now. He left a packet for you. There it is!'

Frodo took the envelope from the mantelpiece, and glanced at it, but did not open it.

'You'll find his will and all the other documents in there, I think,' said the wizard. 'You are the master of Bag End now. And also, I fancy, you'll find a golden ring.'

'The ring!' exclaimed Frodo. 'Has he left me that? I wonder why. Still, it may be useful.'

'It may, and it may not,' said Gandalf. 'I should not make use of it, if I were you. But keep it secret, and keep it safe! Now I am going to bed.'

As master of Bag End Frodo felt it his painful duty to say good-bye to the guests. Rumours of strange events had by now spread all over the field, but Frodo would only say *no doubt everything will be cleared up in the morning*. About midnight carriages came for the important folk. One by one they rolled away, filled with full but very unsatisfied hobbits. Gardeners came by arrangement, and removed in wheel-barrows those that had inadvertently remained behind.

Night slowly passed. The sun rose. The hobbits rose rather later. Morning went on. People came and began (by orders) to clear away the pavilions and the tables and the chairs, and the spoons and knives and bottles and plates, and the lanterns, and the flowering shrubs in boxes, and the crumbs and cracker-paper, the forgotten bags and gloves and handkerchiefs, and the uneaten food (a very small item). Then a number of other people came (without orders): Bagginses, and Boffins, and Bolgers, and Tooks, and other guests that lived or were staying near. By mid-day, when even the best-fed were out and about again, there was a large crowd at Bag End, uninvited but not unexpected.

Frodo was waiting on the step, smiling, but looking rather tired and worried. He welcomed all the callers, but he had not much more to say than before. His reply to all inquiries was simply this: 'Mr. Bilbo Baggins has gone away; as far as I know, for good.' Some of the visitors he invited to come inside, as Bilbo had left 'messages' for them.

Inside in the hall there was piled a large assortment of packages and parcels and small articles of furniture. On every item there was a label tied. There were several labels of this sort:

For ADELARD TOOK, for his VERY OWN, from Bilbo; on an umbrella. Adelard had carried off many unlabelled ones.

For DORA BAGGINS in memory of a LONG correspondence, with love from Bilbo; on a large waste-paper basket. Dora was Drogo's sister and the eldest surviving female relative of Bilbo and Frodo; she was ninety-nine, and had written reams of good advice for more than half a century.

For MILO BURROWS, hoping it will be useful, from B.B.; on a gold pen and ink-bottle. Milo never answered letters.

For ANGELICA'S use, from Uncle Bilbo; on a round convex mirror. She was a young Baggins, and too obviously considered her face shapely.

For the collection of HUGO BRACEGIRDLE, from a contributor; on an (empty) book-case. Hugo was a great borrower of books, and worse than usual at returning them.

For LOBELIA SACKVILLE-BAGGINS, as a PRESENT; on a case of silver spoons. Bilbo believed that she had acquired a good many of his spoons, while he was away on his former journey. Lobelia knew that quite well. When she arrived later in the day, she took the point at once, but she also took the spoons.

This is only a small selection of the assembled presents. Bilbo's residence had got rather cluttered up with things in the course of his long life. It was a tendency of hobbit-holes to get cluttered up: for which the custom of giving so many birthday-presents was largely responsible. Not, of course, that the birthday-presents were always *new*; there were one or two old *mathoms* of forgotten uses that had circulated all around the district; but Bilbo had usually given new presents, and kept those that he received. The old hole was now being cleared a little.

Every one of the various parting gifts had labels, written out personally by Bilbo, and several had some point, or some joke. But, of course, most of the things were given where they would be wanted and welcome. The poorer hobbits, and especially those of Bagshot Row, did very well. Old Gaffer Gamgee got two sacks of potatoes, a new spade, a woollen waistcoat, and a bottle of ointment for creaking joints. Old Rory Brandybuck, in return for much hospitality, got a dozen bottles of Old Winyards: a strong red wine from the Southfarthing, and now quite mature, as it had been laid down by Bilbo's father. Rory quite forgave Bilbo, and voted him a capital fellow after the first bottle.

There was plenty of everything left for Frodo. And, of course, all the chief treasures, as well as the books, pictures, and more than enough furniture, were left in his possession. There was, however, no sign nor mention of money or jewellery: not a penny-piece or a glass bead was given away.

Frodo had a very trying time that afternoon. A false rumour that the whole household was being distributed free spread like wildfire; and before long the place was packed with people who had no business there, but could not be kept out. Labels got torn off and mixed, and quarrels broke out. Some people tried to do swaps and deals in the hall; and others tried to make off with minor items not addressed to them, or with anything that seemed unwanted or unwatched. The road to the gate was blocked with barrows and handcarts.

In the middle of the commotion the Sackville-Bagginses arrived. Frodo had retired for a while and left his friend Merry Brandybuck to keep an eye on things. When Otho loudly demanded to see Frodo, Merry bowed politely.

'He is indisposed,' he said. 'He is resting.'

'Hiding, you mean,' said Lobelia. 'Anyway we want to see him and we mean to see him. Just go and tell him so!'

Merry left them a long while in the hall, and they had time to discover their parting gift of spoons. It did not improve their tempers. Eventually they were shown into the study. Frodo was sitting at a table with a lot of papers in front of him. He looked indisposed – to see Sackville-Bagginses at any rate; and he stood up, fidgeting with something in his pocket. But he spoke quite politely.

The Sackville-Bagginses were rather offensive. They began by offering him bad bargain-prices (as between friends) for various valuable and unlabelled things. When Frodo replied that only the things specially directed by Bilbo were being given away, they said the whole affair was very fishy.

'Only one thing is clear to me,' said Otho, 'and that is that you are doing exceedingly well out of it. I insist on seeing the will.'

Otho would have been Bilbo's heir, but for the adoption of Frodo. He read the will carefully and snorted. It was, unfortunately, very clear and correct (according to the legal customs of hobbits, which demand among other things seven signatures of witnesses in red ink).

'Foiled again!' he said to his wife. 'And after waiting *sixty* years. Spoons? Fiddlesticks!' He snapped his fingers under Frodo's nose and stumped off. But Lobelia was not so easily got rid of. A little later Frodo came out of the study to see how things were going on and found her still about the place, investigating nooks and corners and tapping the floors. He escorted her firmly off the premises, after he had relieved her of several small (but rather valuable) articles that had somehow fallen inside her umbrella. Her face looked as if she was in the throes of thinking out a really crushing parting remark; but all she found to say, turning round on the step, was:

'You'll live to regret it, young fellow! Why didn't you go too? You don't belong here; you're no Baggins – you – you're a Brandybuck!'

'Did you hear that, Merry? That was an insult, if you like,' said Frodo as he shut the door on her.

'It was a compliment,' said Merry Brandybuck, 'and so, of course, not true.'

Then they went round the hole, and evicted three young hobbits (two Boffins and a Bolger) who were knocking holes in the walls of one of the cellars. Frodo also had a tussle with young Sancho Proudfoot (old Odo Proudfoot's grandson), who had begun an excavation in the larger pantry, where he thought there was an echo. The legend of Bilbo's gold excited both curiosity and hope; for legendary gold (mysteriously obtained, if not positively ill-gotten), is, as every one knows, any one's for the finding – unless the search is interrupted.

When he had overcome Sancho and pushed him out, Frodo collapsed on a chair in the hall. 'It's time to close the shop, Merry,' he said. 'Lock the door, and don't open it to anyone today, not even if they bring a battering ram.' Then he went to revive himself with a belated cup of tea.

He had hardly sat down, when there came a soft knock at the front-door. 'Lobelia again most likely,' he thought. 'She must have thought of something really nasty, and have come back again to say it. It can wait.'

He went on with his tea. The knock was repeated, much louder, but he took no notice. Suddenly the wizard's head appeared at the window.

'If you don't let me in, Frodo, I shall blow your door right down your hole and out through the hill,' he said.

'My dear Gandalf! Half a minute!' cried Frodo, running out of the room to the door. 'Come in! Come in! I thought it was Lobelia.'

'Then I forgive you. But I saw her some time ago, driving a pony-trap towards Bywater with a face that would have curdled new milk.'

'She had already nearly curdled me. Honestly, I nearly tried on Bilbo's ring. I longed to disappear.'

'Don't do that!' said Gandalf, sitting down. 'Do be careful of that ring, Frodo! In fact, it is partly about that that I have come to say a last word.'

'Well, what about it?'

'What do you know already?'

'Only what Bilbo told me. I have heard his story: how he found it, and how he used it: on his journey, I mean.'

'Which story, I wonder,' said Gandalf.

'Oh, not what he told the dwarves and put in his book,' said Frodo. 'He told me the true story soon after I came to live here. He said you had pestered him till he told you, so I had better know too. "No secrets between us, Frodo," he said; "but they are not to go any further. It's mine anyway."'

'That's interesting,' said Gandalf. 'Well, what did you think of it all?'

'If you mean, inventing all that about a "present", well, I thought the true story much more likely, and I couldn't see the point of altering it at all. It was very unlike Bilbo to do so, anyway; and I thought it rather odd.'

'So did I. But odd things may happen to people that have such treasures – if they use them. Let it be a warning to you to be very careful with it. It may have other powers than just making you vanish when you wish to.'

'I don't understand,' said Frodo.

'Neither do I,' answered the wizard. 'I have merely begun to wonder about the ring, especially since last night. No need to worry. But if you take my advice you will use it very seldom, or not at all. At least I beg you not to use it in any way that will cause talk or rouse suspicion. I say again: keep it safe, and keep it secret!'

'You are very mysterious! What are you afraid of?'

'I am not certain, so I will say no more. I may be able to tell you something when I come back. I am going off at once: so this is good-bye for the present.' He got up.

'At once!' cried Frodo. 'Why, I thought you were staying on for at least a week. I was looking forward to your help.'

'I did mean to – but I have had to change my mind. I may be away for a good while; but I'll come and see you again, as soon as I can. Expect me when you see me! I shall slip in quietly. I shan't often be visiting the Shire openly again. I find that I have become rather unpopular. They say I am a nuisance and a disturber of the peace. Some people are actually accusing me of spiriting Bilbo away, or worse. If you want to know, there is supposed to be a plot between you and me to get hold of his wealth.'

'Some people!' exclaimed Frodo. 'You mean Otho and Lobelia. How abominable! I would give them Bag End and everything else, if I could get Bilbo back and go off tramping in the country with him. I love the Shire. But I begin to wish, somehow, that I had gone too. I wonder if I shall ever see him again.'

'So do I,' said Gandalf. 'And I wonder many other things. Good-bye now! Take care of yourself! Look out for me, especially at unlikely times! Good-bye!'

Frodo saw him to the door. He gave a final wave of his hand, and walked off at a surprising pace; but Frodo thought the old wizard looked unusually bent, almost as if he was carrying a great weight. The evening was closing in, and his cloaked figure quickly vanished into the twilight. Frodo did not see him again for a long time.